PUFFIN BOOKS

Editor: Kaye Webb

PS 162

THE STREET MUSICIAN

Why should anyone want to dye a large and amiable mongrel dog black? And why should a mysterious blind stranger play one particular gipsy song on his accordion through every street in Louvigny?

To Gaby and his Gang, finding the answers to these questions was a heaven-sent diversion from boredom which provided them with six weeks of intensive sleuthing. But not until they witnessed a heartrending scene in a forgotten street did any of the Ten, with the possible exception of Marion, realize what the real answer to the problem they had set out to solve would be.

Those who have read Paul Berna's classic *A Hundred Million Francs* will welcome another book about Gaby and his friends, and readers who meet these children for the first time will be delighted by this original story, set in the suburbs of Paris.

For boys and girls of nine to twelve years.

PAUL BERNA

The Street Musician

TRANSLATED FROM THE FRENCH BY
John Buchanan-Brown

ILLUSTRATED BY
Richard Kennedy

PENGUIN BOOKS

Penguin Books Ltd, Harmondsworth, Middlesex, England
Penguin Books Australia Ltd, Ringwood, Victoria, Australia

—

First published in Paris as *Le Piano à Bretelle* 1956
Published in Great Britain by The Bodley Head 1960
Published in Puffin Books 1961
Reprinted 1967

—

—

Made and printed in Great Britain
by Richard Clay (The Chaucer Press) Ltd,
Bungay, Suffolk
Set in Monotype Bembo

Contents

CHAPTER I

The Red Lorry

ALL ten of Gaby's gang were sitting in a row on one of the benches in the Square Théodore-Branque, like ten sparrows on a branch. The plumpest sparrow of the ten was half on, half off the very left-hand end.

This was Tatave Louvrier. His right arm was in a sling; that is to say an old pair of braces worn halter-wise held it in its large, none-too-clean bandaging. Tatave leaned lovingly over his arm, and gently rocked it up and down. He

seemed to think there was nothing better in the world than to have one's arm in a sling.

As the nine other sparrows indignantly watched him, they began to sway to Gaby's orders.

'Yo! Heave!' cried Gaby.

'Heave! Ho!' the others replied.

And all together they shoved hard to the left.

The third *heave ho* catapulted Tatave off the bench. He fell like a sack of potatoes, screaming like a stuck pig.

Those on the bench shook with laughter. The girls giggled delightedly and little Bonbon split his sides to see his lumpish brother lying flat on his back on the grass of the square. Other sparrows, real ones, kicked up an equal din all along the Rue du Chemin-de-fer where a playful spring breeze set the fresh lilac that hung over the garden walls dancing.

'Oh! That's a dirty trick!' shouted Tatave, clambering to his feet. 'What about my arm? If you think it's not smashed enough already ...'

'Stop snivelling about your arm, you wrecker!' Gaby indignantly retorted. 'The others don't make half your fuss about a scratch like that. Look at Berthe and Mélie. They're much worse than you. And then there's Zidore. He looks as though a steam-roller had been over him!'

They inspected the casualties. Little Mélie Babin was generally as pretty as a picture, but now she had an ugly black eye and a pair of half-healed scratches down her cheeks from forehead to chin. Berthe Gédéon's head was wrapped up in a saucy gauze turban through which ends of untidy hair peeped. Zidore, too, had come off badly; 'smack on the snout' he would say as he gingerly fingered his bruised and swollen nose. But his legs had suffered worst and they stuck out in front of him, generously daubed with mercurochrome. But they were all undaunted by their cuts and bruises, for at their age things like that did not worry them for very long.

'What a nuisance!' sighed Marion, the girl with the dogs. 'And all because Tatave won't *ever* do things the same way as other people.'

For the hundredth time she was back on the disaster which five days before had destroyed their wonderful horse without a head. Not one of them remembered what had really happened or knew how Tatave had got himself into such a mess. Tatave himself was unable to explain why the three-wheeler had sharply heeled about when it reached the dangerous crossing of the Rue Cécile. The bare fact was that the watchers at the foot of the Rue des Petits-Pauvres had suddenly seen Tatave on the battered horse bearing down the slope *backwards*, their twin cruppers hurtling blindly towards the barbed wire round the Clos Pecqueux.

Tatave's eyes started out of his head, and he howled with fright so hard that he dared not look where he was going or even attempt to avoid his fate by slowing the runaway horse. But their laughter was abruptly smothered when he gave the handlebars that unlucky twist which sent the three-wheeler straight into a group of them.

The wheels had gone right over Zidore; the horse, with Tatave's weight on its back, rolled majestically over him. The right wheel caught Mélie, and the left Berthe Gédéon, and had dragged the two small girls along the rough surface of the Chemin de la Vache-Noire. Unhorsed, Tatave had broken his fall with his right arm, and then bounced head first over the barbed wire. He had made his 'three-point landing' and, pretty well bruised all over, found himself lying among the daisies, frightened, propping himself up on one grazed elbow, and groaning like a cow with stomach-ache.

As for the horse, alas, it had crashed straight into the

concrete telegraph pole at the road junction. Its grey body had split right up the middle like an over-ripe melon and bits and pieces had been hurled in a hundred different directions all around.

'Disintegrated, that's what the horse did!' said Gaby, who was a stickler for the proper word, and whose share had been a bolt which hit him plumb on the jaw.

Fernand Douin had collected exactly ninety-eight pieces of all shapes and sizes, including the back-axle which little Bonbon had kept as a souvenir.

Marion's mother, Madame Fabert, who lived in the house at the corner, had given first-aid to the injured and made a hot chocolate transfusion. To cut a long story short, tears had dried more rapidly than blood.

The gang went into the deepest mourning for their dead and dismembered horse. They felt the real weight of their loss in not knowing what to do with their free time. Of course, they changed the scene of action; the steeply sloping Rue des Petits-Pauvres had lost all its charm after the destruction of their three-wheeler.

After school Juan would lead the whole gang through Petit-Louvigny's jumble of town and country in which he claimed there was plenty of fun to be had. But nothing could come up for long to the high standards of the owners of the battered old horse who had won the highest stakes of the year.[1] Every time the expedition would end in heated discussion on a bench in the Square Théodore-Branque. All day long you could sit and enjoy the busy streets leading to it, and right at the end of the Rue du Chemin-de-fer you could see the suburban trains rattle past or the expresses bound for Paris or Melun.

Berthe and Mélie willingly eased over to make a place for Tatave in the middle of the bench. The ten stuck together

1. See the same author's *A Hundred Million Francs*.

even in their worst troubles. Marion had brought her little yellow dog, Fifi, with her and now she snapped her fingers for it to jump into her lap. It was the gang's mascot.

'What are we going to do?' softly inquired Criquet Lariqué, the Negro boy from the Faubourg-Bacchus.

'Nothing!' Zidore angrily retorted. 'I've sat twiddling my thumbs for the last five days, and every evening it's the same old chorus: go and find something better than the horse!'

The boys sighed deeply. The girls shrugged and pulled faces. The last ride had damped their enthusiasm; they had had enough of the wretched animal.

'What all of you miss,' said Marion in her lilting voice, 'is not the horse itself, it's the business of the hundred million francs which gave us six weeks' real excitement. It doesn't matter about the horse, we've still had the adventure.'

Fernand Douin, owner of the late lamented animal, shook his head sagely as he sat beside her.

'Well?' said Gaby.

'Adventures only happen to people who take the trouble to look for them,' Marion went on with a slight smile. 'Instead of just trailing aimlessly round Petit-Louvigny we'd do much better to get organized. There's plenty going on in the town: let's keep our eyes open, take a good look round and I bet within a couple of days we'll have sniffed out an adventure just as exciting as the one the horse led us into.'

The Ten looked at one another in amazement.

'She's right!' Gaby shouted in a burst of enthusiasm. 'Starting from tomorrow, when we come out of school each one of us'll go off on his own to snoop round one or other part of the town, remembering anything worthwhile he or she sees. At half past six or seven we'll all meet somewhere secret to report what we've discovered. If anyone finds something odd we'll all get on the track of it. Agreed?'

Zidore and Juan rubbed their hands excitedly. This was going to be fun.

'How do you know if something's odd or not?' little Bonbon asked seriously.

Gaby looked angrily at the baby of the gang and tried to keep his temper.

'Listen, Bonbon,' he said sweetly. 'You know old "Spare-a-copper", the tramp from the Place du Marché? Suppose you happen to bump into him on the pavement, what'll he do?'

'Ask me to spare a copper,' answered Bonbon, who could be intelligent on occasion.

'Right. Five minutes later you run into him again. But suddenly you see Spare-a-copper stop beside a lovely blue and white Cadillac, all chromium-plated. The chauffeur whips him a tremendous salute and opens the door. In gets old Spare-a-copper, leans back like a duke, lights a huge cigar, and turns to the bloke, "To the Ritz, Adolphe," he says, "and hurry up about it," and away zooms the car. Well, that's something odd.'

'Gosh!' said Bonbon, his eyes starting out of his head.

He turned to Criquet Lariqué. His mouth agape, the coloured boy was obviously impressed by the example Gaby had chosen. They passed on to other matters.

'Where shall we meet?' Tatave asked. 'They started to pull down the sawmill in the Rue Cécile yesterday. Our shed's gone for good and all.'

'We could meet in the sandpit at Villemarie,' Marion suggested. She knew all the likely spots. 'It's no distance away, just follow the path at the end of the Rue du Remblai and there you are. No one would disturb us and there are a couple of toolsheds we could use if it rains.'

'Good,' said Gaby. 'We'll all get down to it tomorrow. But no fooling about, see! Just remember that to crack a good case without giving the game away you need tact as well as brains.'

Fernand Douin was the only one who had not spoken so far. He could laugh as long and as loud as anyone else, but he was no great talker and the little he did tell the others always showed how carefully he had thought it out and how lively and inquiring his mind was. Now it was enough for him to hear Marion suggest this wonderful idea to get the Gang on the track of an adventure, and he was off in full cry without moving from the bench.

For, by its very position, the Square Théodore-Branque was the ideal spot for the watchful spectator. Through it came the heavy traffic from the main road, the N5, on its way via the Avenue du Quartier-Neuf to the station and the goods depots around it. At set times, too, the railwaymen would use the long Rue du Chemin-de-fer to come on or off duty from the signal boxes and workshops at Le Triage. Then, all day long there was the bustle of Petit-Louvigny's housewives and businessmen to fill the broad pavements outside the shops in the Avenue de la Gare. Finally, on the opposite sides, there was the narrow street, hemmed in by little houses, that twisted away to the no-man's-land of the tramps, the notorious Rue des Estaffiers.

At the junction of all these roads the Square Théodore-Branque provided the loiterer with four comfortable benches on a patch of gravel surrounded by fresh green turf. It was an ideal spot from which to watch people going about their business and the thousand and one exciting things with which the warehouses of a great marshalling-yard are filled.

Fernand spotted a big red lorry speeding up the Avenue du Quartier-Neuf. It belonged to Bollaert, a transport contractor, and he had noticed it at precisely the same time and place on the two previous days. The monster – a twelve-

ton Berliet – braked at the cross-roads. As it passed the
square where the gang was sitting, the driver turned his
head somewhat stiffly and looked closely at them. The fix-
ity of his gaze disturbed Fernand, for it was not the auto-
matic glance to left and right that a careful driver gives. No,
there was something behind the way the man stared at the
children.

From the first the passing lorry had struck a chord in Fernand's brain; why, he did not know. And then there was
something about the driver which he did not like. His
name was Pierce, Paul Pierce, and he had been working for
Bollaert's firm with his brother James for the last few years.
The Pierce brothers were of English origin. They had the
same long horsey jaw, the same florid complexion and they
kept their neighbours at a truly British distance. The happy-
go-lucky Zidore, who knew everyone in Louvigny, reported that they were generous clippers-round-the-ear!

Fernand's eyes followed the lorry to the next intersection.
The red monster swung slowly into the Rue César-Santini
and was lost to view. But Fernand was still with it in
thought, for his natural inquisitiveness prompted him to an
exhaustive study of the whys and wherefores of certain
things. And he knew the locality.

The red lorry slowed down and hooted discreetly twice
as it drew level with Number 43, Rue César-Santini. The
metal blind was up and the long concrete floor of the garage stretched away behind, with three elephantine lorries of
the same size slumbering side by side under the glass roof.
With a blast of its horn to clear the pavement, the new arrival heaved through the entrance. The driver backed it into
line with the others, got out and, seeing the garage empty,
released the counter-weight of the shutter. Down it came
with a rumble and a crash. That was that. Fernand's second
sight went no farther in that particular direction. All he

knew was that the Bollaert firm's lorries generally returned
to base empty.

Carelessly Paul Pierce kicked open the glass-panelled
door to the office. Monsieur Bollaert in his shirt-sleeves was
savagely searching through a bulky file. He was a stoutish
man with black curly hair and a plump, melancholy face
disfigured by a large, stubbly moustache. He looked up and
winked at the newcomer. The driver threw down his re-
ceipts and his logbook on a corner of the desk.

'Everything okay?' Monsieur Bollaert asked absent-
mindedly.

'Not too bad,' his driver answered. 'I got the stuff there in
time. The trouble is that from the twentieth Louvel's won't
accept delivery in the afternoon. I'll have to fix it with James
to do the job in the mornings. It'll only need a dozen trips
to clear their stuff from Platform B. What do you think?'

'We'll see,' Monsieur Bollaert said in the same tone of
voice. 'Anything else?'

'Yes,' said the driver, lowering his voice. 'But it's a different kettle of fish. For the last five days there's been a
darned gang of children on the benches in the square.
When I came back this evening I noticed they were still
there. They looked as though they were up to something.'

'Go on,' said Monsieur Bollaert, replacing his spectacles
to observe the expression on the driver's face.

'Well, it struck me that the Benitez' house is on the
corner of the Rue du Chemin-de-fer. The garden's gone to
seed and it runs pretty close to our back garden. No one
will pay any attention if the kids take it into their heads to
climb over the wall and then they'd have the chance of
sticking their noses in where they weren't wanted. When
kids decide to do something, they do it quickly, and by the
time people start talking it's too late.'

Monsieur Bollaert pushed back his chair, wearily removed his spectacles and gently squeezed the bridge of his nose between forefinger and thumb.

'Don't let's make mountains out of molehills,' he said with a shrug. 'Two years ago we had every reason to distrust the neighbours and local gossip. But the whole business has been dead and buried long ago. Now I've nothing to fear from anything or anybody. You must just keep your eyes open and your mouth shut.'

'That's what I have done,' Pierce answered. 'But you used to keep on at us about being careful. Well, I'm telling you about these kids because they're a bit out of the usual run. Can't you guess? They're the ones who cracked the Paris-Ventimiglia case.'

A gleam of interest shone in Monsieur Bollaert's eyes. He gave a long whistle of surprise.

'Really,' he said. 'Many of them?'

'About ten, including three girls,' Pierce replied. 'The youngest'll be about six and the eldest thirteen or fourteen. What could worry us, boss, is that they've the reputation in the town of being a little too sharp.'

Monsieur Bollaert shook his head.

'Don't worry, just keep your eyes skinned every time you pass the square. Warn your brother and the other two as soon as you can. If the kids decide to come snooping round the house and garden, my wife'll soon be on their tails!'

Pierce was just going when Monsieur Bollaert called him back.

'Incidentally,' he asked him, frowning, 'just what were they playing at?'

'How should I know?' answered Pierce. He wasn't very fond of children. 'Some silly game like any other bunch of kids.'

CHAPTER 2

Criquet and the Small Ad

ON the dot of four the gloomy school in the Rue Piot opened its doors and out poured the children, laughing and shouting. It was a lovely day. Throughout their lessons lovers of the open air had been tortured by the bright sunlight and the fleeting shadows of the clouds. Contrary to habit, Gaby and the others split up on leaving school, each vanishing in a different direction and leaving little Bonbon on his own.

Marion's idea of the evening before had been a magic word, and Bonbon looked at the street with new eyes. It was a wonderfully changed world, in which all sorts of amazing things were going on. The hunt was on. For a few seconds he stared about him and his luck was in, for quite by chance along the pavement came a familiar figure in patched trousers and tattered coat – Spare-a-copper, the tramp. Bonbon trailed him at a respectful distance. He had already made up his mind that sooner or later the old man would give some startling exhibition of his oddness.

One behind the other they slowly made their way up the main street of Louvigny, the Rue de Paris, until they reached the Place du Marché. The street was busy and in twenty minutes ten people paid up without a murmur and another ten as violently refused, which the tramp must have felt to be a pretty fair balance. Bonbon was in ecstasy. He memorized each contribution and each rough refusal and could not get over the unconcerned way in which Spare-a-copper gathered in the cash. When they reached the edge of the square, as Bonbon had foreseen, the tramp cut straight across it and disappeared at top speed inside the Café Parisien. Bonbon had to kick his heels for nearly half an hour and as he waited he cursed the chance that kept the bibulous old tramp gossiping in his heaven on earth.

Spare-a-copper came out of the café, an aura of well-being around his shabby shape. Bonbon took a good look at him and noted that he seemed much more peculiar than before the halt. Perhaps the miracle was about to happen.

He followed the tramp all along the Avenue de la Gare, closing the distance as best the old man's zigzag course allowed. Here and there Spare-a-copper picked up a few more contributions and when he reached the Square Théodore-Branque he unexpectedly swung round. Old man and small boy almost collided on the sun-drenched pavement.

'Gimme a copper!' the tramp demanded aggressively.

'Why should I?' Bonbon retorted, not turning a hair.

Spare-a-copper seemed won over by such frankness. He allowed a smile to creep over his face as he loomed over the fair-haired little boy.

'Sonny,' he said solemnly. 'When you're my age and you've seen life as I've seen it, you'll realize that though a copper here and a copper there don't seem to add up to very much, they're enough to let a man like me who's down on his luck console himself with a glass of red wine.'

'It doesn't look as though it does you much good,' said Bonbon, looking at his tattered trousers and battered boots.

Spare-a-copper did not rise to the affront.

'Why've you been following me about for the last hour?' he demanded icily.

'Did you notice?' said Bonbon, disappointed.

'I notice everything. Did you think I didn't? Ever since

I've been tramping this rotten little town I've had an eye in the back of my head. You need it on this job – got to watch out for the cops. But why've you been following me about, you little spy?'

'You seemed so odd,' Bonbon admitted with disarming frankness. 'And then I was expecting …'

'What were you expecting?' the tramp asked. He was becoming anxious now.

'Why, the Cadillac of course.'

'What Cadillac?' gasped the thunderstruck Spare-a-copper.

'The blue and white Cadillac that's going to take you to the Ritz,' Bonbon explained. 'You don't think I'm going to miss that, do you?'

The tramp's bearded face went one shade redder with surprise.

'I'm wondering which of us is oddest,' he stammered, backing away from this diabolical youngster.

He looked wildly about him and then whirling round he made hot-foot for the station, growling through his beard as though to exorcize the wild idea, 'No, no, no, no.'

Bonbon would have liked to trail him for a little longer, but it was getting late and the others were waiting for him. Thoughtfully he walked back along the Rue du Chemin-de-fer, turned down the Rue du Remblai and hurried off to the sandpit at Villemarie, convinced that, all things considered, Spare-a-copper must be hiding something.

The others were there already. Bonbon and Criquet Lariqué were the only ones missing.

'What on earth can they be doing?' Gaby grumbled impatiently. 'I bet those two kids have upset the whole town with their detective work.'

The gang was gathered on the rickety wooden staging

that overhung a couple of acres of muddy water. By now the sun was low in the sky and the bottom of the pit was in shadow, but the blue sky was superbly mirrored in the stretch of water.

'You'd almost think we were at the seaside,' sighed Berthe Gédéon as she fiddled with her turban of bandaging. 'Another fortnight and we'll be able to swim here.'

'Well, don't drown yourself,' growled Zidore angrily. 'Last year I spent all my time fishing Bonbon out.'

'There's only a couple of feet of water at the edge,' said Mélie. 'Hardly enough to bath a baby!'

On the edge of the pit, sixty feet above them, Bonbon's head appeared.

'Come on!' Gaby shouted impatiently up at him.

There were two ways of reaching the bottom of the sandpit. The girls usually used the ramp that carried a narrow-gauge railway track on which for years a few tipper-trucks had stood rusting. The boys preferred the dangers of a natural Cresta Run worn into the steep side of the pit by the bottoms of the daring few. It was just like a lift; in twenty seconds you were down by the water, but you had to roll smartly to one side if you wanted to avoid getting in the back the half-hundredweight of sand you had brought avalanching down behind you. The slide was fun, but unfortunately those who had ridden the late, lamented horse-without-a-head had higher standards.

Bravely Bonbon launched himself down the slope and burst like a shell into the middle of the gang. From their long faces he gathered that their search too had been just as unrewarding as his.

'What did you find?' Gaby demanded.

'I followed Spare-a-copper,' Bonbon announced importantly.

'Well?'

'I did my best, but it wasn't any good. The old chap isn't ready for the miracle yet.'

This simple view of things cheered them all up. The older boys admitted their failure. Appearances had deceived Gaby, Zidore, and Spanish Juan as well. They, too, had trailed victims as devoid of mystery as the brazen old beggar of the Place du Marché. Two patient hours' shadowing had convinced them that there was no dark secret beneath old Zigon, the rag and bone merchant, Monsieur Galli, the shoe-mender of the Rue des Petits-Pauvres, or Raise-the-Dead, the local postman. Their unimportant lives were so ridiculously commonplace that fate would never have any adventure in store for them.

Mélie Babin had brought her scouting to bear upon the cashier of Lalouette's Bank and had caught him in a cul-de-sac peering through the ventilator of Macherel's bakery. She waited for him to go and had then taken his place at the peep-show. She bent over to see Monsieur and Madame Macherel going for each other hammer and tongs in the gloom of the bakehouse. It was interesting, but a family row did not get them much nearer a real mystery.

The idle Tatave had felt the best thing to do was to go to the fountainhead of the mysterious. He had 'picked up' Inspector Sinet of the local police as he left the station and from a safe distance had escorted him on his beat, without being seen. This in itself was quite a feat. His patrol had ended in a quiet café in the Rue Casimir-Bompain. Three large men were playing 'belote' with an obvious lack of enthusiasm. Sinet had watched the game over their shoulders for a moment and then obligingly offered to make up the fourth.

'Louvigny's a dead-end!' Tatave ended despairingly. 'Nothing ever happens. Why, if Inspector Sinet himself just

twiddles his thumbs and plays cards, how do you expect us to get on the trail of anything interesting?'

'Inspector Sinet and Commissioner Blanchon don't necessarily handle the best cases,' said Marion, trying to raise her friends' morale. 'There are probably other ones, which aren't exactly criminal, so the police don't interfere. And one of those is what we want to discover.'

'Hi,' came a voice above them.

Criquet Lariqué was on the edge of the cliff. He went down on all fours and began to feel his way backwards down the slope. All his endeavours to preserve the seat of his trousers were, however, in vain. Halfway down, the incline took command and delivered him to the gang in a fog of tawny sand.

'If you go on coming down like that,' Gaby told him indulgently, 'you'll have the whole cliff on us one of these days. Got some good news for us, Cricri?'

The Negro lowered his head and spread out his hands innocently.

'I met my mother on the corner of the Rue Piot,' he said in a sad little voice.

'And you'd nothing better to do than follow her home,' said Zidore amid general laughter. 'You should have tried to race her.'

'Couldn't do anything else,' Criquet admitted despairingly. 'She'd got me by the hand. I'd like to have seen you ...'

The gang howled with mirth. Though Madame Lariqué was built on formidable lines she was as nippy as a centre-forward, as Gaby had found to his cost. One evening the year before, he had brought Criquet home with his best trousers more or less in shreds. The first pair of blows had found their mark on Criquet's head. Gaby had tried to take to his heels, but the coloured woman had caught him and nearly twisted his ears off. But Criquet had not finished his story.

'All the same,' he said, 'I did find something.' He searched his pockets.

At once the laughter ceased and a ring formed round him. He carefully smoothed out a piece of torn newspaper.

'It's an advert,' Criquet explained. 'I only just spotted it when I was reading to old Monsieur Loubat, the neighbours' grand-dad. You know him, he's only got one eye. Here, Gaby, you read it. I've put a cross beside it.'

There was a reverential hush as Gaby took the paper and read out what it said:

Disabled man in poor circumstances would adopt good house-dog. Strong, intelligent, well-trained, affectionate and able to get used to new owner quickly. Breed unimportant. No dealers. Apply Monsieur Théo, 58 Rue des Estaffiers.

The end of the advertisement was lost in the clatter of a goods train along the embankment above them. Gaby had to pass the paper round from hand to hand for them all fully to appreciate Criquet's sensational discovery. But the bitter laughter and the disappointed remarks were ample comment.

'Where did you get it?' asked Zidore.

'From this week's *Louvigny Express*.'

It was the local newspaper. Criquet awaited his leader's decision.

'It's very nice of you, Cricri,' Gaby said kindly, 'but your advert doesn't help us. Just what did you see in it?'

'I ... I ... don't know,' stammered Criquet. 'I thought it a bit odd. It isn't just an ordinary advert.'

'It's just the thing for Marion,' said Zidore. 'You'd be only too glad to get rid of one of your hounds, wouldn't you, Marion?'

Marion nodded happily.

'Of course I would,' she said and smiled at Criquet. 'And I've one that ought to be just the thing – Nanar. A car on the main road hit him. But he's got over it now and he could be quite useful to someone like that. I'll take him along tomorrow morning, as it's Thursday and we won't be going to school.'

'Watch out,' said Juan. 'That Rue des Estaffiers isn't

exactly healthy. You're not going there alone. I'll go with you, and Zidore and Fernand'd better come too. We'll see just what sort of a fellow this Monsieur Théo is. After all, it might lead us to something, you never know. What do you think, Gaby?'

'You don't want to miss anything,' the leader of the gang said, without committing himself. 'Go if you like. We'll meet at eleven in the Place du Marché as usual on Thursdays.'

It was time to go home. In single file they climbed the narrow-gauge track, helping one another over the trickier bits. Marion's little dog, Fifi, bounded along in front, while Gaby brought up the rear. He shouldered the clumsy Tatave up the incline and looked as though he was supporting the entire party. The sun sank in a crimson ball behind the hazy horizon. In the distance the trains sped through Le Triage, with a clatter and a roar that filled their ears like a storm at sea.

As they crossed the Square Théodore-Branque, Juan and Criquet Lariqué dropped out of the gang and turned towards their homes in the Faubourg-Bacchus. The others split up at the Place du Marché. Only Marion and Fernand headed for the Rue des Petits-Pauvres. At first they walked in silence, Fifi playing at their heels.

'A funny thing happened to me this afternoon,' Fernand muttered after a minute or so.

'Why didn't you tell just now?' asked Marion, surprised.

'The others would only have laughed at me,' Fernand answered. 'And in any case they were all so keen to tell their own stories.'

'That's no answer. Tell me.'

'All right,' said Fernand. 'I've noticed for some time that we aren't exactly everybody's favourites. Some people don't like us at all. Why? I just don't know ... Do you know that big block of buildings on the corner of the Rue César-Santini and the Rue du Chemin-de-fer?'

Marion did not interrupt. She was quite carried away by the dramatic undercurrent of Fernand's story.

Like the others he had left school at four o'clock and had gaily walked away on his own until he came to the Square Théodore-Branque. There was not a soul there. He had noticed that Bollaert's lorries did not return to their garage until six or half past, which left him plenty of time. Hands in pockets, kicking a stone in front of him, he went on to the corner of the Rue César-Santini. He glanced quickly round. The road was quiet and unfrequented. The houses were new and set widely apart, each surrounded by a large leafy garden. Here lived the notables of Louvigny and the aristocrats of the meat trade. Number 43 stood out from the rest by its length and by the height of its windowless frontage. From a distance Fernand made sure that the garage doors were open and that none of those tough characters in greasy overalls, pillars of the firm of Bollaert, was in sight.

Strolling on, he approached by the pavement opposite. It was the wisest thing to do. Monsieur Bollaert's car, an aged Renault perpetually in need of a wash, was parked between the door leading to the office and another that gave on to the back garden. Fernand had never seen the latter open. He walked on and, since the street was still quite empty, he crossed and slowly approached the garage. The four red lorries of the Bollaert fleet were out for the moment and the glass-roofed garage seemed all the larger for their absence. Fernand's nostrils were assailed by the smell of diesel oil and rubber which the building exhaled.

He stopped at the threshold, pressed himself against the wall, and peered in. Nothing stirred. Nor at first sight was there anything suspicious. The mystery lay, not on the oil-

stained concrete floor, but rather in the complete silence
that reigned in the garage and its environs and the house
adjoining. The movement, the muted bustle of a successful
business were totally lacking and yet Bollaert & Company
were supposed to be working to full capacity.

Fernand would very much have liked to take a look at
the workshop-cum-store that opened off from the end of
the garage. But to do so he would be putting himself in the
wrong. And yet was he not in the wrong already by spying
on people who had never harmed him? Fernand ignored
the question and plucked up enough courage to go a little
way into the garage.

From there he could see more clearly the dimly-lit store
in which a dozen great oblong packing-cases bound with
metal strips were stacked. Fernand was gripped by a fever-
ish curiosity. He went still farther into the garage and tiptoed over the threshold of the store, his head flicking from
left to right like some small prowling animal.

Click! He had only brushed the metal blind, but down it
came like a game-trap with a thunderous crash that shat-
tered the stillness of the garage. Fernand did not dare move.
He heard heavy footsteps approaching over the concrete
floor.

'We've got him,' said an angry voice which must belong to one of the Pierce brothers. 'A fat little rabbit.'

Two people laughed. The other must be Monsieur Bollaert. Fernand knocked timidly on the door.

'Let me out,' he begged.

'All in good time,' said the man calmly. 'I'm going to
keep you there a little while to teach you not to trespass on
other people's property.'

Chuckling, he walked away. Fernand resigned himself to
wait in patience. But for how long? This was serious. He
had lost all interest in what the mysterious packing-cases

might contain, and was on the verge of tears. Thank goodness the others could not see him caught like a rat in a trap.

Five minutes later the unhurried footsteps of the man returned. He listened, and hearing nothing, pulled up the shutter. It was James Pierce, the driver. He was apparently some years older than his brother, for a lock of white hair escaped from under the dirty old cap on his head.

Tongue-tied, Fernand came out with lowered head. Monsieur Bollaert was standing in the office doorway to watch the criminal go by.

'What were you looking for in here?' he asked threateningly. 'I watched you coming down the road, looking as if butter wouldn't melt in your mouth, you young devil!'

'I wanted to see the

lorries close to,' was the first answer that came to Fernand's
mind. 'I'm awfully interested in lorries.'

The two men burst out laughing.

'That's a good one!' cried the driver, taking a firm grip
on Fernand's collar. 'You couldn't even get the bonnet of
one of our Berliets into the corner where we caught you.
Now get out! The next time I catch you down our street I'll
give you something that'll put you off lorries for the rest of
your life!'

He dragged the boy to the door and helped him on his
way with the toe of his boot. Hot with shame, Fernand ran
off and never looked back until he reached the Rue du
Remblai.

'The way those two carried on gave me cold shivers,'
Fernand admitted as he reached the end of his story.
'The others wouldn't have come out of it any better,
not even Gaby. Do you think there's anything in their
stories?'

'A lot of hot air,' laughed Marion.

'Mine's got much more to it than that. Something funny
is going on in that place on the Rue César-Santini. Look,
don't you think they may be up to something just as big as
the Paris-Ventimiglia business?'

Marion shook her head reprovingly.

'You haven't lost your nose for this sort of thing,' she
said softly, 'but you shouldn't have gone into Bollaert's
place just like that. They're on their guard now and it'll be
terribly risky to investigate the garage again.'

'Well, should I tell the others?'

'Leave it,' Marion answered. 'They'll soon find something less dangerous. But don't you ever go down that
street unless there are several of us with you.'

She gave Fernand a quick hug, whistled for her dog and
then she was off. Fernand watched her vanish round the

corner; then he went home. His was the first house in the Rue des Petits-Pauvres, right on the corner.

After all the excitement he was glad to be back in the little house. It was not very grand, but he was the heir-apparent there.

Monsieur Douin was sitting by the window reading his newspaper as he waited for his young son.

'This is a fine time to come home!' he grunted as he put up a stubbly cheek for a kiss.

'We've found a wonderful new game,' Fernand explained, unabashed. 'But you've got to work at it and that takes time.'

'You'd do better to work at that,' Monsieur Douin retorted dryly, pointing to the satchel hanging behind the door. 'Your mother won't be back until eight. Now, get on with it.'

Fernand spread his text and exercise books on the table, scratched his head a moment, and less than twenty minutes later he had solved a tangle of equations that would have tried the temper of a saint.

Monsieur Douin, meanwhile, gently sucked his pipe and gazed affectionately at his son. When he saw that he was out of the mathematical maze he asked in pretended mockery, 'What's this new game you've thought up?'

Fernand was not taken in. He told him all about the gang's first investigations, but took good care not to say a word about the mystery he had uncovered that afternoon.

'Lord,' Monsieur Douin sighed, and raised his eyes to the heavens, 'what will you be up to next? I bet that business of the horse has gone to your heads. Oh, I know you were sharp and you handled it well, but you did have luck on your side. It was a million to one against the police being fools enough to let a gang of kids turn up a hundred million francs right under their stupid noses.'

CHAPTER 3

The Mysterious Monsieur Théo

MARION dressed herself in her best clothes to go to 58 Rue des Estaffiers. She wanted to make a better impression than her pet, the famous Nanar.

For Nanar was a mixture of all the long-haired breeds, although he carried his spaniel's head with its great liquid eyes proudly. If the advertiser was not particularly concerned about the pedigree or colouring, as he claimed, then all should be well. Nanar's coat was reddish, with black and grey patches, the whole stippled with gold. He was extremely well-behaved, but it would have been hard to find an animal as ugly as he.

'Let's hope I'm not too late,' said Marion to the self-effacing Madame Fabert, her mother. 'The *Louvigny Express* came out yesterday morning, and Monsieur Théo may have had several answers already. The one thing that keeps me hopeful is that he wants a big dog and Nanar fills the bill there.'

As she dressed she indulgently watched the huge hound chase Fifi round the room and send the chairs flying. Outside, at the bottom of the garden, the girl with the dogs could hear her other lodgers barking jealously from their wooden kennels.

Once April was over, Marion shed the man's jacket that she wore in cold weather and came out in print smocks, rather short in the skirt, which gave her long, wiry, restless legs their freedom and made her look prettier and slimmer. But for special occasions she kept a dark-blue dress which brought out her delicate complexion, her pale gold hair, and the light in her grey eyes. Her twelve-year-old vanity was satisfied by a gilt brooch which Fernand had spent two hours choosing from the shilling dip at a fair.

Marion was just pinning on this brooch when the three boys arrived. They, too, had made some effort to smarten themselves up, even Zidore, who was usually the most disreputable member of the gang.

'Ready?' asked Juan.

'Give me another five minutes,' said Marion. 'I must brush old Nanar just once more.'

The others used the delay to wheedle a cup of chocolate out of Madame Fabert. Meanwhile Marion ran a metal comb through the monstrosity's particoloured coat, brushed his ears, muzzle and the tip of his tail, which plumed out beautifully.

'Fancy *giving* away a dog like that!' Zidore muttered from the depths of his cup. 'What rotten luck! And after you'd fed him for six months too! Your Monsieur Théo isn't half doing well out of the deal.'

'Don't you believe it!' Marion answered with a wink. 'He'll feel the pinch: that dog's going to cost him something in food alone, he wolfs down four or five pounds of food a day. Hi, Nanar!'

She tied a piece of string round his neck and the four children set off happily in the fresh light of morning, Fifi trotting at their head.

They took a short stroll round the Thursday market on the square in front of the station and then they made off down the Avenue du Général-Cahin, despite Fernand's suggested short cut. Marion guessed the reason but kept quiet. Fifty yards ahead their path crossed the Rue César-Santini. Fernand put on a spurt when they reached the junction; he had not got over his fright of the previous afternoon. None the less he could not help glancing towards Bollaert's garage. The four red lorries were drawn up outside, ready to go to the goods-yard, and completely blocked the narrow street. The Pierce brothers and their minions bustled about them and there was a hum of idling motors. Fortunately the pavements were full at that hour of the morning and the four children and their two dogs were lost in the throng.

Marion had kept the advertisement and now she frowned as she read it while they walked along.

'Monsieur Théo!' she said suspiciously. 'That's not what I'd call a *real* name.'

'I've never heard of him,' Zidore said. 'And yet I bet I know everyone round here. Of course if you live in a road like that you're likely to be a pretty shady character.'

'I spoke to dad last night,' said Spanish Juan. 'He thinks this Monsieur Théo is a retired railwayman or something like that.'

'Disabled man in poor circumstances,' Marion read. 'That doesn't get you very far, does it?'

'It means he's minus a hand or two so he can't even reach into his pocket to pay for Nanar,' laughed Zidore. 'It's a useful trick. Why, I could put in the same sort of advert: *Orphan in poor circumstances would adopt sturdy bike in good working order with all accessories. Make unimportant. No dealers. Apply: Monsieur Zidore, 45 Rue du Malassis. The little door under the stairs.*'

They roared with laughter.

'That *would* be something to do,' said Fernand. 'Pity adverts cost so much.'

'That's what makes me rather wonder,' said Marion. 'Everyone in Louvigny knows I look after lost dogs and find homes for them. If Monsieur Théo hasn't heard of me, it either means he's new to the district or else he's scared of showing his face.'

'We'll soon see,' Zidore interrupted. 'Come on, hurry up. We don't want to find dozens of people with dozens of Nanars all waiting when we get there.'

Juan guided them straight along the main road; the houses began to thin, with vacant lots or overgrown cul-de-sacs between them. Soon they were looking down on the tramps' no-man's-land, a dismal tangle of untidy fields and tumbledown sheds of plasterboard or corrugated iron.

'Here we are,' said the gipsy boy.

They turned left at the cross-roads and the Rue des Estaffiers was before them. It was dark, there was no pavement and its greasy cobblestones twisted away between dilapidated houses and rickety sheds from whose depths came the cackle of hens. It was the home of the poorest of Louvigny's poor, and of its worst characters, so people said. You had only to see the expression on the faces of the young gentlemen who wandered from bar to bar in their slippers, caps pulled down over one eye, to know they were right.

'What's that you've got, a dog, a goat, or a tiger?' one of them asked Marion and pointed at Nanar.

'Grrououou!' Nanar replied.

The children had their first shock when they reached Number 58. For someone 'in poor circumstances' a two-storey house standing in a well-tended garden with a tile-roofed outbuilding alongside seemed rather grand.

'You could house a regiment in that palace,' said Zidore indignantly.

Marion rang the bell of the garden door. A few seconds later they heard the sound of slow footsteps within.

'Who's there?' a harsh voice demanded.

'I've come about the advertisement,' Marion answered. 'Is that Monsieur Théo?'

A door opened a crack to disclose a burly, bald-headed
man in homespun, khaki jacket and corduroy trousers. He
seemed quite surprised to find four children and two dogs
standing outside his front door.

'I am Monsieur Théo!' he announced. 'Now, what do
you want?'

'I've brought you a lovely dog,' said Marion. 'I'm sure
he's just what you want. You'll be quite satisfied with him.'

Behind her, the boys nudged one another. They had

expected to see the disabled man of the advertisement, but Monsieur Théo had fists like hams, legs like tree trunks and the aura of strength his massive form exuded was quite frightening. 'Retired railwayman, or something of the sort,' thought Zidore, who also felt sure he scented the atmosphere of prison around the ageing giant.

'Which do you mean, the big one or the little one?' asked the unsmiling Monsieur Théo as he watched Fifi and Nanar playing around.

'The big one, of course,' laughed Marion. 'He's just what the advert asked for.'

'I hope he's not dangerous,' said Monsieur Théo.

'Don't worry,' said Marion. 'He's a good dog. Here, Nanar, say hullo to the gentleman.'

The enthusiastic Nanar bounded forward, set his fore-paws on Monsieur Théo's chest and licked his face.

'I can see he is,' said Monsieur Théo, gasping for breath and wiping his moustache with the back of his hand.

The boys were beginning to fidget in the background. Zidore's face had taken on that look of fixed stupidity that betokened he was bottling up laughter.

'Good,' snapped Monsieur Théo, and held out his hand. 'Give me the lead; I'll take him in.'

Marion jumped back.

'Just a minute! I'm not going to give you Nanar until I know how you're going to look after him and if you'll feed him properly. I don't want to find him all skin and bone on the street corner in a fortnight's time.'

Monsieur Théo's eyebrows came down, and they were black and bushy. Obviously he was beginning to lose his temper.

'The dog's not for me,' he growled threateningly.

'I didn't think he was,' Marion politely replied, looking the giant up and down. 'The advert said a disabled man.'

'But I can promise you your Nanar'll have an easy life,' Monsieur Théo went on. 'Now, give me the lead and get it over and done with.'

Marion was still undecided. Zidore and Juan had stolen to one side to see what they could see through the door. All that was visible was the corner of the kitchen garden and the door of the outbuilding, which was tight shut. Not a sound came from the house. Monsieur Théo was becoming impatient.

'Are you keeping him or giving him away?' he asked Marion, tapping his foot impatiently. 'It doesn't matter to me if you keep him. I'll have the choice of a couple of dozen before the day's out. Well?'

Then he must have sensed Marion's indecision.

'What are you scared of?' he asked more gently. 'I want him for a blind man. You've never seen a blind man ill-treat a dog, now have you?'

This final plea made Marion feel sorry. She passed him the lead. Nanar changed hands without any trouble.

'He had a good feed this morning,' said the girl, not wishing to leave anything to chance. 'He needs at least three a day. And no scraps either, a good half-pail of bread and bones. You know, something solid. Nanar's a good watch-dog and he'd rather sleep out of doors.'

It was obviously a big wrench for her to give away the animal she had rescued when he had been abandoned, injured, by the roadside. On the verge of tears, she added in a sad little voice:

'He hasn't got fleas.'

Seconds passed as Monsieur Théo looked through half-closed eyes from one to the other of the four children. A slight smile lifted the tips of his waxed moustaches. However, Marion did not expect him to say thank you.

'Here, Nanar!' said Monsieur Théo, tugging at the lead.

Surprised, the dog turned and looked at Marion. But she did not wait. She ran off as fast as her legs could carry her so that no one should see how upset she was. The boys politely raised their berets before they went and Fifi merely cocked a leg against one of the doorposts. Monsieur Théo looked thoughtful as he watched them go.

'Well, there's a home found for another of them!' Zidore exclaimed as he and the two others caught up with Marion. 'But I bet you have a replacement for him in your zoo in a couple of days.'

'What did you think of old waxy?' asked Juan.

'He looked like a retired wrestler,' Zidore retorted. 'I shouldn't like to meet him on a dark night round the corner of the Rue des Estaffiers. Marion was dead right, he's the sort that's not too keen to show his face.'

'While you two were looking inside,' said Fernand, 'I noticed how he was on the verge of coming down on your necks. He's a tough character, Monsieur Théo is.'

'What did you see?' asked Marion.

'Nothing very much,' Zidore answered. 'Everything was neat and tidy, but what interested me was that out-building alongside the house. All locked and bolted, and iron bars over the windows.'

'Keep moving,' Fernand said to the others. 'I don't like the look of the natives.'

Folk in the Rue des Estaffiers glared at the four children as they passed.

'Hi!' called the young man in the cap who had spoken to Marion earlier, 'what have you done with your zebra?'

They hurried on without replying. Harridans with their hair in curlers turned to stare in hostility as they went on their way. An urchin accompanied them to the cross-roads, heaping them with choice epithets that were not current in the Rue des Petits-Pauvres.

'We shouldn't have got all dressed up,' said Zidore. 'I'd have felt much more comfortable in my old pair of trousers.'

They were relieved to see the familiar main road before them and soon they were in the safety of the Square Théodore-Branque. Marion had just enough money to buy a round of chocolate buns.

The four sat munching on one of the benches in the square, and went over what had happened bit by bit.

'Poor Nanar,' sighed Marion, staring blankly before her. 'They'll beat him black and blue.'

'Don't worry!' said Zidore. 'They won't turn him into sausage meat.'

Of the two, Marion was nearer the mark, though she had no idea of the tiny bit of truth in what she had said.

As soon as the door of number 58 Rue des Estaffiers closed behind the children, that of the outbuilding opened. Filling the doorway was a man, tall and burly as Monsieur Théo, wearing a clinging, striped seaman's vest. A long-peaked blue cap was pulled down over his eyes and he chewed the stub of a cigar.

'Well?' he asked Monsieur Théo.

'We've found just the dog we want first shot,' said Monsieur Théo, showing Nanar to him. 'At all events he's the right shape and size. What do you think?'

The other man inspected Nanar and scratched his stubbly chin.

'He's the wrong colour,' he said, after a moment or so. 'The poor brute looks more like a rainbow.'

'We'll soon fix that,' said Monsieur Théo. 'Call the others.'

The man poked his head into the building and gave a piercing whistle. A few moments later out came two disreputable figures of indeterminate age, rubbing their eyes.

'Fetch me the two big tin tubs from the dormitory,' Monsieur Théo told them. 'Sacco, you bring that new tin on the shelf in the workshop. And fetch two pounds of soap flakes. Get two baths ready, one for washing and one for dyeing him. I need a really splendid black dog.'

Monsieur Théo's men bustled round the yard. Nanar half-realized what they were going to do to him and would have raised some sort of objection. But Monsieur Théo gripped the lead firmly and the dog gave in to his new master. Besides, there was a kindly look in his eye as he scratched Nanar's ears in a way that showed he really was fond of dogs.

Half an hour later, after one last rinse under the tap, a different Nanar escaped from the hands of his tormentors. Monsieur Théo, his henchman, Sacco, and the pair from the dormitory laughed like children as they admired his new coat. It shone coal-black and his yellow eyes sparkled below the tufts of hair.

'Get him a meal,' Monsieur Théo told Sacco. 'And see there's a good chunk of beefsteak in it. He's been as good as gold and he should have his reward. That's the way to do it.'

No one seemed to take any notice of a fifth man half-hidden in the dormitory. Monsieur Théo automatically glanced in his direction. From the room came a tremulous broken little tune. At first it was no more than a scattering of notes that conveyed the player's roving fancy. Then the tune itself became more and more plain as chord followed chord and soon the building re-echoed to the boom of the accordion. The four men listened, their heads to one side. Nanar's ears had pricked up and his eyes were riveted on the door.

'Let him go,' Monsieur Théo told his friends.

The dog moved inquisitively into the doorway, muzzle pointing to the far end of the dormitory, tail gently wagging. Then he went straight in.

'He's gone all by himself,' said Monsieur Théo contentedly. 'That's a good sign.'

CHAPTER 4

A Useful Lead

JUST before midday on the Place du Marché Gaby and the others heard what had happened earlier that morning. Marion's glum looks made all the boys try to be as kind as possible.

'It's the sort of case we've dreamed about,' said Gaby. 'And it's starting to take a really peculiar turn. But when you look at it, it was Cricri who gave us the lead yesterday evening by bringing us that advert everyone laughed at.'

The coloured boy beamed with pleasure. The gang was in full force on the end bench in the square, facing the Café Parisien.

'You say that Monsieur Théo can't often show his face outside,' Gaby went on. 'That doesn't matter 'cos we've a friend in their camp now – Nanar! All we need do is follow the dog every time he goes out, whoever's with him, and maybe he'll lead us into an adventure.'

Gaby had only put forward his plan to reassure Marion that they would all keep an eye on the animal she held so dear. She had no objection to the scheme. But Zidore and Juan had, although they were the boldest element in the gang and often sailed pretty close to the wind. The two 'hard cases' now wore expressions that would have done credit to a high-class funeral.

'All very well,' said Zidore, 'but first of all I'd like to know just how you mean to run this business. I'm not going home every night all mucked up and with a bloody nose into the bargain.'

'The Rue des Estaffiers,' Juan added in tones of high tragedy, 'is like enemy territory. It's easy to go in, but you can never be sure of getting out again with a whole skin.'

'Poor little things!' cried Gaby, and burst out laughing. 'Who said we were going to war with them? At first we'll simply watch all the exits from the street. Little Bonbon can do that as easily as anyone else.'

'Where does the Rue des Estaffiers begin?' Tatave asked, still nursing his damaged arm,

'At the bottom of the Rue Tournante, near where it crosses the main road,' Zidore answered.

'And where does it end?'

'At the top of the Rue Tournante,' Zidore added with the same assurance.

'But that's silly!' said Berthe Gédéon. 'A road can't begin and end in the same road.'

'Haven't you ever been outside your own back garden?' chuckled Zidore. 'Look! The Rue Tournante is one of the oddities of the district. Every time we go to the sandpit we pass the first houses in it in the middle of the Rue du Remblai. As you can see from its name, the Rue Tournante turns back on itself two or three times and it cuts the Rue des Estaffiers in three different places. It's quite simple. Here, look.'

With his finger-tips he roughly sketched the layout in the dust of the pavement. The others got off the bench to peer over his shoulder.

'This is really going to be some game,' said Gaby, bubbling with excitement. 'Listen to me! From two o'clock onwards my H.Q. will be in the Square Théodore-Branque. Tatave, Berthe, and Mélie will stay with me. Their bandages make them too noticeable and get in their way. They'll be my dispatch riders, so they won't miss any of the fun. The other six will split up into couples and they'll watch at the three exits from the Rue des Estaffiers. Look.'

He put his finger on Zidore's sketch map. The others crouched down to see more clearly.

'Now, listen carefully,' said Gaby, lowering his voice. 'Here's the bottom end of the Rue des Estaffiers, where the Rue Tournante cuts it for the first time. It's only about five hundred yards from the Square Théodore-Branque. Marion and Fernand will occupy Observation Post No. 1. A little higher up the Rue Tournante cuts the Rue des Estaffiers for the second time, almost in the middle. Zidore and Bonbon'll hide near the junction. It's just by Number 58, so they'll be able to watch Monsieur Théo's house and still keep in touch with the post lower down. Finally, Juan and Criquet will stand guard at the other end of the road where the Rue Tournante cuts it for the last time. Juan and Cricri will keep in touch with Zidore and Bonbon. If something happens at the top of the street at Post No. 3 Juan will send Cricri right away to Post No. 2. Zidore will send Bonbon to Post No. 1 and either Fernand or Marion will bring the news to me at my H.Q. in the square. If you look sharp I'll know within five minutes what's going on at the front and then I can give you the necessary orders.'

'What a lovely game!' said Bonbon happily.

'At each of the three posts,' Gaby added, 'one or both of the watchers, at least, will know Monsieur Théo. So if he appears, with or without Nanar, we mustn't lose track of him. We've got to be careful how we organize the pursuit, so that we don't put Marion, Zidore, Juan, and Fernand to the fore, because he knows them already.'

In the bright sunshine the Ten eagerly discussed their plans. There was already a holiday atmosphere about the Place du Marché, where a fresh breeze strained at the stall-holders' multi-coloured tents. They were still at it when a silent shadow loomed over their circle. Gaby was speaking, but he stopped abruptly and began to play with a handful of gravel. Marion and Zidore half turned. It was Inspector Sinet, with his battered old black hat, his bottle-green trench-coat, and his long horse face.

'What are you up to now?' he asked suspiciously.

'Just drawing the squares for a new game of hop-scotch,' Zidore, who always had an answer, replied.

They moved back so that he could see the plan. Inspector Sinet frowned and stared in complete bewilderment at the criss-cross pattern traced in the dust. He could not recognize in it the plan of a district into which his professional duties often took him.

'How on earth can you play with silly games like that?' He shrugged. 'You *do* disappoint me.'

'It may not look much, but it's just as good as a game of "belote", Mr Inspector, sir!' Zidore retorted, his voice heavy with meaning. 'Wouldn't you like us to show you?'

The Gang broke into a roar of laughter. Inspector Sinet did not understand and took good care not to search for the hidden meaning. He turned sharply on his heel and beat a dishonourable retreat.

'You can't be very bright to let an oaf like Tatave follow you around for an hour and still not notice,' hissed Gaby as he followed the Inspector with a hostile glare.

As arranged, the observers were at their posts by two o'clock. It was very hot and they took refuge in the shade of the walls or in the cool of the side roads and innocently amused themselves. The whole length of the Rue des Estaffiers was calm and peaceful. Gaby and his three casualties passed the time by telling detective stories to each other as they waited on the bench in the square.

At about half past two Juan decided to test that the

system was working properly. He spotted old Zigon coming down the Rue des Estaffiers with his handcart full of empty bottles. Off he sent Criquet Lariqué to Post No. 2 with the news. Only too happy to cause Gaby a false alarm, Zidore dispatched Bonbon to Post No. 1. The smile on his face as he trotted up reassured Marion and Fernand, who entered into the scheme enthusiastically. Off shot Fernand hell for leather down the main road and roared into the Square Théodore-Branque. Gaby jumped up excitedly from the bench as he saw the breathless runner approach.

'Old Zigon sighted five minutes ago at the top of the road,' Fernand called to him. 'It's only a practice.'

Gaby kept calm.

'I should have thought of it myself,' he said. 'Let's wait for him. Then we'll know how long, on the average, it takes to get here.'

Two or three minutes later there was a clatter of bottles as the old man came into the square. Twenty yards behind him Bonbon strolled along, hands in pockets, head in air. Seeing the others had taken the quarry in charge, he turned and vanished as he had come.

Gaby rubbed his hands.

'It works! This is going to be marvellous,' he told Fernand. 'Now, back to your post and keep your eyes skinned.'

Soon after three the Rue des Estaffiers awoke. They had to keep doubly on the alert and to repel the approaches of the young 'Estaffiers' who haunted the vicinity with their dull games. A nine- or ten-year-old urchin circled Zidore and Bonbon suspiciously.

'What are you kids doing here?' he demanded arrogantly. 'You don't belong to this street. Hop it and be quick about it.'

'Take a running jump at yourself,' Bonbon retorted smoothly.

Zidore kept quiet. He watched the young 'Estaffier' through half-closed lids and fondled three large stones he had collected in case of trouble. The urchin saw them. He also saw Zidore's legs – striped with scratches and glistening with mercurochrome. A hero's legs. Wisely he retreated. But he had been enough to distract Zidore's and Bonbon's attention for a few seconds, and in that time a man had come out of Number 58. Slowly he approached them; with him was a big black dog on a lead. Zidore and Bonbon had not seen him open the door of Number 58 and close it behind him and so they let the two pass them without another thought.

'That's a lovely dog,' said Bonbon.

The man wore a blue cap with a long peak and a striped seaman's vest, and he peacefully chewed the stub of a cigar as he murmured endearments to his dog.

He strolled to the end of the road right under the noses of the look-out men at Post No. 3, Criquet Lariqué and Juan. Criquet even put out his hand to stroke the dog, without having an inkling that Nanar was within his grasp.

Fifteen minutes later the door of Number 58 opened once more and this time Zidore and Bonbon were on the alert. At once the former recognized the towering shape of Monsieur Théo and sent Bonbon hot-foot to Post No. 1. Anxious to save time, he himself ran over to Post No. 3 to warn Juan and Criquet. The three then set off on a roundabout route towards the Square Théodore-Branque whither Monsieur Théo was wending his way.

Fernand's expression warned Gaby at once that this was the real thing, even before the former reached him.

'Monsieur Théo's coming down the street,' Fernand breathlessly announced. 'He's alone. No sign of Nanar!

He's wearing a Basque beret, black coat, and light-grey flannels. You'll spot him easy as anything.'

'Run back quick and warn Marion and the others,' Gaby told him. 'Wherever he goes we'll be on his tracks. All afternoon if we have to.'

'The others know. Everyone's coming back as fast as they can.'

'Right. Wait for them on the corner of the square. You six take cover at the top of the Rue du Chemin-de-fer. And take care not to let him see you! If Monsieur Théo recognizes you he's bound to be suspicious. I'll stay here with the other three. He's never seen us, so we can pick up the trail as soon as he appears.'

Two minutes later an unsuspecting Monsieur Théo came into the square from the main road and passed the mouth of the Rue du Chemin-de-fer without noticing six children huddled in a convenient doorway. He took the shortest way across the square, ignoring the pedestrian crossing, and made his way round the grass plot in the middle. There was a great lout of thirteen or fourteen pretending to saw the head off another young oaf who had his right arm in a sling. Two little girls with scratched faces were active spectators of the scene and were urging the executioner to saw still harder. Tatave had his neck across the back of the bench and was sticking his tongue out a frightening distance. Monsieur Théo saw it all out of the corner of his eye, found the children's general appearance particularly stupid, and was quite satisfied in his own mind that they really belonged to Louvigny-Triage. Then he strode on along the Rue Casimir-Bompain towards the Grand-Rue.

Gaby gave him fifty yards start, then he let go of Tatave's neck and signed to the two little girls. All four of them raced away on the tracks of Monsieur Théo, slipping like Redskins between the passers-by. At once the other six came out of hiding and followed the first group, pairing off with a ten-yard gap between couples. The whole manoeuvre went like clockwork. As he crossed the Grand-Rue Monsieur Théo looked back, but he could see nothing unusual in the crowded pavements. None the less ten pairs of keen eyes fiercely followed his every move.

'I hope to goodness he doesn't take us out to Louvigny-Cambrouse!' said Gaby to Tatave. 'We'd have to follow him in the open and then things really would become tricky.'

But instead of turning left towards the allotments, Monsieur Théo kept straight on for the fine new building on the corner of the Rue Cécile.

The Ten, meanwhile, had joined forces on the pavement. Jaws gaping in shocked amazement, they watched a turn of events as unsportsmanlike as it was unexpected. Monsieur Théo flicked his cigarette-end down a drain, greeted two policemen cycling back from their beat, and vanished behind them into Louvigny's Central Police Station.

'He didn't half lead us up the garden path,' Gaby cried in consternation. 'It's no game now.'

'Let's wait a bit,' said Marion.

So they loitered in the vicinity for a good half hour, one eye on the pictures outside the Eden Cinema, the other on the entrance to the Police Station.

Then Zidore could stand it no longer.

'We're not hanging round the Police Station all afternoon,' he said indignantly. 'Any minute now the cops are really going to sit up and take notice. Can't you see how crazy we are? Sinet himself only has to look out of his office window and he'll spot us. Let's give it up for today and go to the sandpit; we could all do with a paddle. My poor feet feel as though they're dropping off.'

Gaby and the others made the mistake of falling in with the suggestion. But it *was* hot and they couldn't waste a whole Thursday holiday waiting for a so-and-so who had the freedom of a police station.

Away they went, gaily casting the blackest suspicions on Monsieur Théo's activities.

CHAPTER 5

A Tune on the Accordion

HARDLY ten minutes after they had gone, Monsieur Théo came out of the Police Station with a most unprepossessing couple. Each carried a small cardboard suitcase of the cheapest sort, and without a word he led back the way he had come and let them in at last through the garden door of Number 58 Rue des Estaffiers.

'Here we are!' he exclaimed. 'You can stay as long as you like. There aren't very many of us at the moment and there are plenty of spare beds. But watch it! No nonsense, mind. I'm not having any trouble with the rest of the street!'

The character called Sacco had just come back from a walk with Nanar. He came over and shook hands with the newcomers who stared about them with amused curiosity.

'If you're not bone idle,' Monsieur Théo went on, 'you'll soon pick up casual work in the goods-yard at the Junction, while you're waiting for something better to turn up. I'll see that you get on your feet again.'

'You see,' the burly Sacco added, 'we're all one family here.'

Monsieur Théo nodded.

'All pals together,' he said. 'But don't forget I'm the boss!'

They chatted for a minute or two and then the door-bell rang.

'That'll be Popaul and Lofty,' Monsieur Théo told Sacco. 'Let them in.'

The two characters who had aided in Nanar's transformation came into the yard. Lofty was a tall creature with a mean pasty face around whose bony frame hung ill-fitting denims, Popaul a jovial, red-faced little man, in a pair of faded blue overalls.

'Oho! We've got reinforcements,' said Popaul with a wink.

Monsieur Théo ceremoniously introduced the newcomers to the residents, and soon they were talking together in a friendly manner and slapping one another on the back.

'You'll take these two in hand for me,' Monsieur Théo told Popaul and Lofty, 'and start straight away unless they've got too soft in prison! I don't like idlers round my place.'

'All we want's a job to do,' said one of the newcomers. 'We aren't afraid of work, are we, Toto?'

Monsieur Théo looked pleased.

'That's what I like to hear,' he said, 'because I mean to give you an extra little job. If you do it as I want it'll be a way of paying for your board and lodging.'

The door of the outbuilding was ajar. Evening shadows were filling the empty building, but an accordion played unceasingly, the notes rippling on like a stream.

'Who's that?' asked one of the newcomers with evident curiosity, jerking his thumb towards the dormitory.

'A poor sort of chap,' Sacco answered. 'But he's going to play the lead in our little business.'

The sun had set before the gang returned from the sandpit. Being a Thursday, their families had supper much later, so as to let them make the most of the day of freedom. Criquet Lariqué and Juan were in no hurry, so instead of dropping off at the Faubourg-Bacchus, they were only too

glad to go as far as the station with the others. And so it was
that all ten of them were back on the same bench they had
occupied that morning before setting out on their man-
hunt. It had proved a failure, but a disappointment like
that was unlikely to put a final damper on children so re-
sourceful as they. In the calm of the evening there was renewed enthusiasm for the most hare-brained schemes.

'Of course,' said Gaby, pulling a face, 'it's a rotten shame
that that clown should be well in with the police. First time
anything goes wrong we'll have every copper in Louvigny
on our tails.'

'That'll make it all the more exciting,' cried Zidore.
'We'll have the fun of leading the police up the garden
path. They get so bored with their brand new police station
they spend their time playing belote.'

Gaby scratched his head.

'Shall we go back to our posts round the Rue des Estaffiers, then, tomorrow evening after school?' he asked the
others.

Everyone said yes. But Fernand leaned forward to cast a
questioning look at Marion. Within the Gang itself theirs
was a closer and more personal friendship. But Marion's
expression was set, her eyes were far away and she seemed
to be listening to something else. Fernand nudged her. She
did not move. She had heard above the rumble of the
traffic, above the clatter of the junction a strange sound
coming from behind the sooty station buildings. It was
not unpleasant.

'Listen!' she suddenly said, raising her hand. 'There's
music coming from the Rue des Petits-Pauvres.'

They pricked up their ears for a moment. Yes, they really
could hear a faint tune above the roar of the expresses and
the scream of their whistles as they rushed through the
station.

'It's the juke-box in the Bar-Tabac,' said Zidore. 'It's the only one in the district.'

'A juke-box?' exclaimed Marion indignantly. 'Are you all deaf?'

'Let's go and see, that's the most sensible thing to do,' Gaby suggested.

They all went off together. It was like the good old days of the horse-without-a-head.

The music was really coming from the Rue des Petits-Pauvres. Seized by curiosity, they walked on until they could hear the wheezing notes of an accordion playing at the bottom of the road. The housewives stood watching at their front doors, the expression on their faces matching the melancholy air from the instrument.

The musician was sitting on a camp stool on the corner of the Rue Cécile. It was hard to see him clearly, for that part of the street was already in the evening shadows.

As they approached, Marion and her friends noticed a big black dog crouched against his knees and, on the pavement in front of him, a battered old tin for contributions. So far all it held was a solitary ten-franc piece.

With his head thrown slightly back, the musician played away at an old accordion. Its keys were yellow with age and the bellows worn at the creases. He himself had on an ancient black overcoat going green along the seams, black trousers frayed at the ends, and a black hat with a floppy brim. A pair of dark glasses half hid his haggard face.

'He's blind,' said Bonbon, in an awed whisper.

A shyness they could not explain held the Ten back and they all stood on the pavement opposite. The blind man played a little bit of everything and played it well: 'pop' tunes, old-time waltzes, half-forgotten favourites. The sound of his accordion filled the narrow street, and its echoes gave it a charm it had not known for many years.

Marion stared enthralled at the black dog, and the black dog's yellow eyes stared back at Marion. Its bushy tail gently stirred the dusty pavement. Marion did not dare move. For the first time she began to have some inkling of the real implications of the affair in which she had involved her friends.

Fernand turned towards her.

'See?' he whispered. 'That black dog...'

'Sh!' said Marion. 'Don't tell the others. At any rate not for the moment. They could wreck everything. Yes, it's Nanar all right. I'm so glad.'

Nanar gave a little whine, and strained at his leash to reach Marion. The blind man let go of his accordion with one hand and softly stroked the dog's head. Nanar subsided at once and obediently

sat down beside the camp stool. He seemed quite devoted to his new, blind master.

'I always thought he was the best dog I ever had,' Marion murmured unselfishly.

After about ten minutes the blind man seemed to get tired and stopped playing. The ten-franc piece was still the only money in his tin. The children were kind-hearted. Automatically they turned to Marion as the Gang's treasurer.

'We spent a lot on the shadowing yesterday afternoon,' she said regretfully. 'Ten ice-cream cornets at twenty francs a time. It's a lot of money. All we've got in hand is one fifty-franc piece.'

'Give it to him,' said Gaby.

Slowly Marion crossed the street and deposited the coin in the tin. The blind man never said so much as thank you, but Marion felt he was staring hard at her through his dark glasses. Nanar's hair bristled with affection as he felt his benefactress furtively stroke him.

Gaby was no fool. He had as sharp a pair of eyes as Fernand or Marion and her gesture opened them. One thing still puzzled him. That morning Nanar had led them to Monsieur Théo, himself a puzzle, and that evening had, as it were, laid at their feet the blind man, whom no one had ever seen in the district before. In the meantime Nanar had undergone this strange alteration which added yet another element of mystery to the case. Fernand's thoughts were running on the same lines, as he told himself that Nanar's transformation alone raised a problem with many unknown facets to it. What reasons had prompted the turning of Marion's particoloured monstrosity into such a beautiful black dog? That seemed the key to the whole business.

Marion returned to her place with the Gang.

The blind man paused a moment and then took up his

accordion once more as if to give the Rue des Petits-Pauvres one last tune. In a different key, and with perhaps a little more feeling behind it, he broke into an old gipsy air which soon cast its throbbing spell over the narrow street.

The listening housewives were affected by the music, but not so deeply as to go indoors to see if they could spare a few francs from the housekeeping money. Marion, Berthe, and Mélie listened with rapt looks on their faces, for the melody had a hidden charm that went straight to their soft hearts. The boys, who were made of sterner stuff, stayed on the alert.

'I know that tune,' Tatave said confidently. 'It's called *Pour deux sous d'amour*. I've heard it five or six times on the radio. It's pretty old.'

Gaby had turned to whisper in Zidore's ear. The Terror of the Rue du Malassis' eyes opened wide and he stared hard at the blind man's dog. Then his pale, hungry face split in silent laughter.

'Know the man?' whispered Gaby.

Zidore shook his head.

'Not at first sight,' he answered, carefully watching the odd couple. 'He must be new to the place. But look, if Nanar's disguised why shouldn't his master be too? Let's have a closer look.'

'Not yet!' hissed Marion. 'We don't want to wreck everything.'

The secret had passed down the line, from one to the other until even Bonbon knew.

'Stand still and shut up!' growled Gaby to the less re-strained members of the Gang. 'Or I'll twist your ears off. We're really on to something now and we don't want to lose it all by acting stupidly. A little patience is what's needed. Crikey! A mystery you could solve in a couple of minutes wouldn't be worth while.'

The blind man's concert was over. He shut his accordion up and, slipping the straps off his shoulders, set it carefully down beside the camp-stool. Then he picked up the tin, tipped out the two coins and put them in his pocket. After that he waited motionless, his hands clenched round the top of his white stick.

The girls were still under his spell. They stood there, heads cocked, as though the echoes of the music still reached them above the dull murmur of the junction.

'He's a jolly odd sort of blind man!' said Zidore, still concentrating on externals. 'You'd think he was just playing for his own amusement. It can't be a very paying proposition in a poky little back street like this. What do you think? He's been here a quarter of an hour and all he's picked up is sixty francs. Old Spare-a-copper'd have made ten times as much without any trouble at all.'

Night was falling over the town, the setting sun crimsoned the rooftops but the street was in darkness. The blind man sat motionless on his camp-stool.

'Hang on for a minute,' said Fernand. 'Something's sure to happen.'

Two or three minutes passed and then someone came hurrying round the corner. The children saw at once that it was the peanut seller from the Place du Marché. 'Monkeynuts', as he was called, walked down to the cross-roads and seemed relieved to find the blind man sitting in the shadows. The latter got up and slipped the accordion over his shoulder without a word, while Nanar wagged his tail happily. Monkeynuts took charge of the stool and the tin. Then the blind man put his hand on his companion's shoulder, tugged at Nanar's lead and all three of them slowly made their way back towards the station.

It was too late to do anything, but Juan and Criquet

Lariqué had to take the same direction to get back to their homes in the Faubourg-Bacchus.

'Don't you worry, we'll follow him to the end of the road,' Juan told his friends as he took Criquet by the hand. 'It's everyone's supper time so I don't suppose those two will lead us to the ends of the earth. See the rest of you to-morrow.'

Reluctantly the Gang broke up. They almost felt that, having scented a mystery, it would be gone by the next day.

'I'm going home,' Marion told Fernand. 'If something fresh turns up, let me know.'

As she went down towards the Chemin de la Vache-Noire by herself she unconsciously hummed the haunting tune that had just come into her head – *Pour deux sous d'amour*.

CHAPTER 6

Monsieur Bollaert Takes Fright

THE first council of war was held the next day during the nine o'clock break under the four lime trees that cast their meagre shadow on the school yard.

At last they could all hear the results of Juan's and Criquet's shadowing.

'Monkeynuts steered the blind man as far as the Square Théodore-Branque,' the gipsy boy told his ring of friends. 'He left him on the corner of the main road and the blind man went on all by himself with Nanar. Cricri and I followed him at a distance right along the Rue des Estaffiers. The blind man must be beginning to get to know that part of the route because he went straight up and rang the bell at Number 58 – Monsieur Théo's place!'

'We expected that,' sighed Marion. 'We're no farther forward than we were last night.'

'What if we ignored Monsieur Théo and concentrated on the blind man?' Gaby suggested. 'He's much easier to watch, and if there isn't something mighty queer about him, then I'm a Dutchman.'

'Sure,' said Zidore. 'So you think he's not strolling round the neighbourhood just for the fun of it with a dog dyed black!' This made everyone laugh.

'Let's concentrate on the blind man,' Marion agreed.

'Good,' said Gaby. 'When we come out of school we'll go straight to the square. We'll send reconnaissance parties out from there in all directions. Louvigny isn't as big as all that, and wherever the blind man's playing his accordion we'll soon know. From then on we'll split the job between us. We'll take it in turns to shadow him. We mustn't lose sight of him for a minute.'

But well before school ended, the blind man woke the ten spies with a start as they drowsily bent over their books. It was nearly three o'clock when they heard the accordion echo down the Rue Piot. Monsieur Juste was busy at the blackboard, but he could not help noticing the current of restlessness that flowed from certain of his pupils, good and bad alike, whom he had written down as 'difficult'.

Gaby, Zidore, Fernand, and Tatave felt their hair bristle when they heard the lively little tune above the noise of the traffic. As if to rub it in he played successively at each of the four corners of the block that held the school.

Red with frustration, Gaby bit his lips and stared at the clock.

'This is the limit!' Zidore cursed impatiently. 'What earthly use is it telling us that the square of the hypotenuse equals the sum of the squares of the other two sides? Fat lot of good that is! All the time Nanar and his mate are just slipping through our fingers.'

Boldly, Tatave raised his hand, quite undismayed to be disturbing Monsieur Juste at the blackboard, and, pretending to be in distress, asked to be excused. When he returned five minutes later he whispered to the others that the blind man was going away towards the Grand-Rue. And in fact by this time the accordion was silent.

A moment later they could hear it a little farther off, but it was so faint that the squeak of the chalk on the blackboard drowned its trills and flourishes.

Fernand had remained calm. Seemingly he was absorbed in the mysteries of that holy-of-holies, the hypotenuse. In fact he was busily copying, on a larger scale, a little street map of Louvigny given away by one of the big stores. He had had the idea at the back of his mind for some time. The little plan was quite clear, and Fernand took a lot of trouble to reproduce the smallest cul-de-sac and the scattered groups of houses stretching away towards Petit-Louvigny. Satisfied that his task was properly done, he carefully folded the map and slipped it into his hip pocket. He was to value the piece of paper as highly as if it were the map of a treasure island.

When school finished the main gate seemed all too narrow for the stampeding Ten. They had not far to run. As they stood on the corner of the Rue de Paris waiting to cross the road so as to take the shortest route down the Rue Casimir-Bompain to headquarters in the square, Marion halted them.

'There it is; he must be at the bus depot,' she said, pointing down the street. 'Can't you hear him?'

Jostling one another in their haste, they made their way down the main road. Where it joined the Rue de Paris a wide parking space had been made and this was used as a terminus for the buses to and from Paris. As these came and went almost uninterruptedly all day long, the place was full of people.

The blind man had taken his stand on one of the narrow islands between the buses, with Nanar sitting a little behind him to the right of the camp-stool. The tin was not yet overflowing with money but it seemed to be coming in faster here than on the corner of the Rue Cécile. A few idlers had gathered round him and were listening with obvious enjoyment.

There was no question of the children being so rash as to swell the scanty audience. Gaby gave Fernand and Marion detailed instructions before leaving them there, while he and the others went back to the square. From there he sent Juan and Zidore to take possession of that corner of the Rue

Tournante which they had used as Post No. 2 the day before and from which it was easy to watch Number 58, Rue des Estaffiers. Having made his disposition, Gaby calmly waited to see what would happen next. Every ten minutes he sent a runner in one or other direction to keep his forces busy.

Marion and Fernand chose an empty bench at the end of the island, not far from the blind man, from which they could watch him without a bus blocking their line of sight every other minute. They both had their satchels with them and now they bent over their schoolbooks with pretended studiousness, all the while keeping one eye on the other end of the island. The blind man would pause between tunes more or less briefly, stroke Nanar's shaggy head, and crane his head this way and that as though trying to pick out one special sound among all those of the bus depot.

Twice running during the course of the next half-hour, dispatch-rider Bonbon came racing up the Rue de Paris, circled the watchers twice and thumbed his nose at them in respectful greeting.

Towards five o'clock Fernand noticed the bony form of Monkeynuts on the other side of the depot. The old man circled the crowd, basket on arm, croaking his wares. He took his time and did not appear to pay the slightest attention to the blind man. Finally his way led him to the bench on which the children sat. He plumped heavily down beside them, and began to complain bitterly how little appetite the townspeople showed for his nuts.

'And yet I get them direct from Saint-Louis in Senegal,' he said, turning sharply towards his neighbours. 'Yes I do! Go on, try one.'

Fernand and Marion chewed their peanuts politely. Fernand took enormous care not to refer in the old man's presence even obliquely to the musician or to the tunes he was playing, for he did not want to rouse the suspicions even of that unimportant figure in the mysterious business.

At that very moment up popped Bonbon and stood and gaped to see his friends deep in conversation with Monkeynuts. He turned on his heel and raced off to the square.

'News!' he told Gaby. 'Monkeynuts has just come into the bus depot. He's sitting next to Fernand and Marion.'

'What are they doing?'

'Chatting away like old friends and eating peanuts,' said the outraged Bonbon. 'It's not right!'

'You little fool!' Gaby retorted in a rage. 'You should have stayed down there. You beat it just as something was going to happen. Stay here, you get too worked up. I'm sending Berthe Gédéon instead.'

Meanwhile a second character had taken his stand on the island a yard or so away from the blind man. The children knew him well, he was Amédée, the newspaper seller, a tall fellow with a twitching face, who always wore a cap. Amédée watched the buses come and go as he waited for the first edition of the evening papers. At first Fernand paid no attention to him, he was so much a piece of the landscape, but then he noticed Amédée's mouth open every so often. While pretending to watch the traffic he was saying something very fast and each time he did so the blind man gently nodded his head as he went on playing his accordion.

A newspaper van suddenly swung at top speed off the main road and pulled up alongside the island. Its arrival set things moving. Amédée leapt for the door of the van: the driver flung a great pile of papers on to his waiting arm and whispered something in his ear. A moment later Amédée glanced round and, noticing Monkeynuts standing a little to one side, he signed to him to come over.

The three men had a brief discussion and then the van roared off. Amédée slipped half the papers into the bag which hung at his side and took the rest over to the woman who kept the nearby paper stall. Then he walked off towards the station, making the Rue de Paris ring as he shouted out his 'Evening papers'. The blind man must have realized what was going on around him, for he slipped his arms out of the accordion straps. Monkeynuts came over and tapped him gently on the shoulder. Keeping hold of Nanar's lead, he got up and the procedure of the previous evening followed like a well-learned lesson.

It was Berthe's turn to put in an appearance. She saw the pair on the pedestrian crossing over the main road, and then Marion and Fernand leisurely getting up and fastening their satchels. Fernand made a distant signal to her with his hand. The little girl understood at once and turned to run and warn Gaby.

To his immense satisfaction the latter was given news from both directions at the same time, for Zidore, too, came running from the Rue des Estaffiers with a choice morsel.

'Two men just came out of Number 58, going towards the station,' he told Gaby. 'Couple of pale-faced miseries, thin as laths, wearing frayed suits. They don't look as though they know their way about the district and they've gone off down the Rue Tournante. Juan's left the Observation Post to follow them. He'll meet us here in half an hour unless his shadowing produces results.'

A little later Marion strolled into the square from the Avenue du Quartier-Neuf.

'The blind man is playing in the courtyards and passageways of the Cité-Ferrand,' she told the others. 'Monkeynuts steered him over to the first block of flats and now he's gone back to the Place du Marché as usual. I left him sitting on his bench outside the Café Parisien. It looks to me as though the old chap is only in this business as a guide for the blind man.'

'That's quite likely,' said Zidore. 'After he's been taken around like this for a fortnight, the blind man should be able to find his way around the district on his own. Shall I relieve Fernand?'

'No!' said Gaby in tones that left no room for argument. 'It's not worth drawing attention to ourselves just for the fun of making the game more complicated. Anyway Fernand keeps his eyes skinned and if there's anything to see, he'll see it.'

Four fine, horseshoe-shaped blocks of flats made up the Cité-Ferrand. They had been built near the station for railwaymen who had lost their homes in the war. Between them ran short private roads, closed to traffic, and each block faced south towards the town over a courtyard-cum-garden planted with acacias and Lombardy poplars. The courtyards were ideal playgrounds for the children from the flats, and Fernand was a trifle embarrassed to find that his presence at once roused the curiosity of a number of his friends from school.

'Want a game?' one of them suggested, pointing to a patched old football.

Fernand unwillingly agreed. But it was the only way of explaining what he was doing in this well-populated quarter where the Ten had often been involved in skirmishes. He began to kick the ball about with a dozen other keen novices of the game.

A few feet away the blind man played in the corner of the courtyard. There he sat for nearly a quarter of an hour, working away at his accordion with an energy that Fernand judged to be ill rewarded. As he got up the opposing team very conveniently scored a final goal through a first-floor window.

There was a clatter of glass and the players scattered like

a flock of sparrows amid a storm of angry imprecations. Fernand, taking advantage of this, slipped away to follow the blind man into the neighbouring passageway.

Here the accordionist played for a long while, ringed by an audience of silent little girls. Fernand sat on a doorstep a little way away and pretended to be half asleep, though he missed nothing of what happened in the street. All seemed so peaceful, so comfortingly normal that the boy began to wonder whether Marion and the more enthusiastic supporters of the game had not let their imaginations run away with them. Perhaps a very simple explanation could dispel the cloud of mystery with which they had so unthinkingly invested the blind man. Of course, there was the inexplicable transformation of Nanar: on that Fernand had to admit defeat.

What had he gleaned from his first turn at shadowing? Very little. In the first place the blind man had rechristened his dog. Fernand had noticed this quite by chance. Nanar's lead had come untied from the camp-stool and the dog had padded over to be patted by the little girls. At once the blind man had sensed his companion move and had called him back in a croaking voice: 'Toby!' Nanar answered just as well to his new name and returned to crouch obediently at his master's feet.

Fernand was equally struck by the way the accordionist selected his tunes. Each time he took up a fresh position the blind man would break into a series of different airs which he would play with hardly a break between them. Next would come a fairly long pause of some two or three minutes during which he would sit absolutely still. Then he would pick up his instrument once more and would play that haunting gipsy melody, with its undertones of sadness, that the children had first heard in the quiet of the Rue des Petits-Pauvres – *Pour deux sous d'amour.*

It was only when he was in the middle of the Cité-Ferrand in the second passageway that Fernand noticed this peculiarity, and the long silence that in some way separated it from the tunes that had gone before. This procedure made him suspect a secret purpose: it was as though the street musician was trying to put across a signature tune to his audience on the pavements, at the windows and in the doorways.

With the same precaution Fernand followed him into the last courtyard. He felt his interest revive. The blind man planted his camp-stool against the wall, placed his tin in front of him and crashed into an ascending scale that brought every key of his old accordion into play. Then he vigorously began his usual selection of popular tunes.

Fernand listened attentively, but at the same time he closely watched the passers-by in the next street. In the distance he heard the growing roar of a heavy lorry coming up the Rue Ponceau in bottom gear. His head turned and he saw one of Monsieur Bollaert's red monsters heave into view round the bottom of the road.

The heavy lorry slowed down as it drew level with the flats in the Cité-Ferrand. Fernand was already crouching behind one of the fat pillars of the doorway. He had recognized the long, red face of Paul Pierce behind the flashing windscreen. As he passed the last block of flats the driver automatically looked round and saw the blind man sitting in the courtyard facing him.

Fernand was watching like a hawk and he noticed the look of blank amazement that crossed Paul Pierce's ugly face. The lorry went on, but a moment or so later the screech of brakes drowned the accordion. Fernand crouched even lower, sitting back on his heels, his face between his hands, as though he were half asleep.

People were hurrying down the Rue Ponceau. Some

turned right into the courtyard, and gossiped as they walked towards the staircase of the flats, Fernand raised his head a little and saw Paul Pierce among them. He was strolling carelessly towards the doorway, his thumbs in the shoulder straps of his blue overalls.

The driver stood in the doorway and looked around him. He did not notice the urchin crouched in the dust, but his eyes strayed towards the accordionist and Fernand heard him catch his breath in alarm.

Paul Pierce stepped a little closer still to the blind man and for a moment pretended to be absorbed by the music. Then he hurried back the way he had come and vanished in the crowd. Two minutes later Fernand heard the lorry start up and disappear noisily towards the station.

It was half an hour before Juan returned to Headquarters in the Square Théodore-Branque.

'I shadowed them to the goods-yard,' he said disconsolately. 'The couple from the Rue des Estaffiers joined the men waiting for the "A" Siding to open. They queued up with the rest at the little office to get their cards and at five o'clock they were on the job with the others shifting the stuff.'

'What stuff?' asked Gaby, pricking up his ears.

'Lord! What you usually find in a goods wagon – barrels, sacks, crates. That's all.'

Zidore looked up.

'It's one of those inside jobs,' he said with a sniff. 'Those two are stooges. They've been put there to tip off the arrival of a really valuable consignment. When a sealed wagon comes into Louvigny they'll shift the stuff all right – into their own pockets!'

Obeying orders to the letter, Fernand reached the rendezvous at half past six. His face did not betray his feelings.

'We aren't the only ones interested in the blind man,' he said casually. 'And we'd better not meet here any more. We'd give ourselves away as soon as anything happens if we did. I'll tell you why.'

He told them of his earlier misadventure in Monsieur Bollaert's garage and then detailed the results of his shadowing. They were all badly shaken by the entry into the case of the formidably-built figures whose four red lorries traversed the town. Gaby, Zidore, and Juan had long known, both by sight and reputation, Monsieur Bollaert's drivers and Monsieur Bollaert himself.

'It's all to the good,' said Juan, 'because I don't suppose they'll take much notice of us three.'

'We don't know that,' Gaby answered gloomily. 'First thing to do is to find somewhere out of the way for our headquarters. The sandpit at Villemarie's too far away, so don't suggest that.'

Each one put forward the most likely place they knew, but it was Marion who once again carried the day, for she had not forgotten any of the requirements of such a hideout.

'In the middle of the Rue du Remblai there's a turning called the Impasse des Otages,' she said. 'That's where those people were shot in 1944. There's seldom any traffic in the Rue du Remblai because it doesn't lead anywhere. But there we'll be the same distance from the Rue des Estaffiers, the Place du Marché, and the Rue César-Santini. We want to think of that.'

The gang at once evacuated the Square Théodore-Branque. There was little hope of their return, for the benches were much too exposed to the view of the enemy.

'I wonder what's behind it all,' said Gaby as he strode away.

'What do you think?' Zidore retorted sarcastically.

'Money. Just like the Paris-Ventimiglia business. And these men are hunting high and low for it. That's all people think about these days.'

'It would be a shame if it were!' Marion said gently. As ever, she expressed the better feelings which the others seldom put into words.

Things were at a standstill at Monsieur Bollaert's garage. Paul Pierce jumped down from his lorry and swept into his boss's office like a tornado.

'He's back,' he said dully. 'I've just seen him. A couple of minutes ago.'

Monsieur Bollaert's fat, pasty face went green. He could not speak at first.

'It can't be,' he said, wiping his hand across his face. 'You must have been mistaken.'

'I saw him as plain as I see you,' said Paul Pierce. 'And I'm sure I wasn't mistaken. You don't forget a face like his in a hurry. He was playing his accordion down by the Cité-Ferrand. And he still has his big black dog with him. Take the car down there if you don't believe me. You'll soon see I haven't dreamed it all up.'

Monsieur Bollaert sagged back in his chair, unable to stand up to the blow.

'Do something,' Paul Pierce anxiously advised him. 'Tip the police off. You mustn't let him get you down like this.'

'What's the use?' sighed Monsieur Bollaert. 'He's free to play his accordion all over the town if he likes. All I can do for the moment is to move my wife and the kid to the little house in the Rue Bout de l'An. I bought it on the quiet, so nobody knows I own it. I'll go back to them every evening. There, at any rate, we shan't be disturbed.'

'That doesn't solve your problem,' said Paul Pierce. He

shook his head. 'All you're doing is making your own life impossible.'

'I'm going up to see my wife,' said Monsieur Bollaert, unwilling to listen to him. 'Back your lorry into the yard and get hold of the others as quick as you can. We'll start moving right away.'

'And what about those kids, always thinking up more mischief on the benches in the square?' Paul Pierce growled and slammed the garage door behind him.

They worked well into the night in dead silence behind the locked doors of Monsieur Bollaert's garage. Part of the furniture left the house and disappeared into a great red lorry.

CHAPTER 7

The Detectives' Club

It needed nearly a fortnight's shadowing, as close and as scrupulous as Fernand's, to get some definite news about the blind man and to fix his daily routine. Although Marion, Zidore, Juan, and Gaby particularly distinguished themselves in a task which required quick-wittedness as much as patience, each of the others, however small or unskilful, added his personal touch to the portrait of the blind man.

Every evening after seven the duty shadower made his report to the meeting of the Detectives' Club at the bottom of the Impasse des Otages. Gaby would write down the vital information in the little laundry book which never left his shirt pocket.

The new headquarters were in a grass-grown alley closed by the wall of the gasworks. A black marble tablet and a few faded wreaths commemorated the twelve Resistance men who had fallen before a firing squad. Ten years after the event the wall still bore the marks of the bullets. But these tragic symbols did not affect the children, nor did their laughter desecrate the half-forgotten place of death.

Bonbon's report gave them their first clue to the blind man's name.

The apparent innocence of his age (he was only six) was disguise enough to enable him to shadow the blind man from very close range, and one day he was close enough to be within hearing distance when Monkeynuts was steering him through the winding streets near the church.

'Here we are, Monsieur Anatole,' the kindhearted old man had said as they stood at the corner of the Rue des Alliés. 'You just keep straight on for the Chemin de la Vache-Noire. You'll know when you get there, the surface is so bad. On your left there are four little side streets, but you'll have no trouble crossing them. At eight o'clock I'll come and pick you up again.'

Even Bonbon was impressed by the deferential way in which Monkeynuts spoke to the blind man. The latter growled something in reply and went off, his white stick tapping the edge of the pavement.

'Monsieur Anatole!' Gaby groaned. 'Every single person in the case seems to be hiding under a false name. There must be six dozen Anatoles at least in the district. That's not much help.'

'Hang on! I found out his real name too,' Bonbon added hurriedly. He never gave all his news away at once. 'All the stallholders in the Place du Marché call him "The Phantom".'

The older children burst into hoots of laughter and Bonbon had to be told just what picture the name conjured up in people's minds.

'Anyway it's as good a name as any other, and it fits him very well,' Gaby admitted, laughing. 'The market people generally hit on the right nickname for someone whose face they don't like. So let's call the blind man the Phantom!'

'I had a very, very close look at the Phantom,' Bonbon added. 'I was nearly breathing down the back of his neck. He's got quite a few white hairs, he must be awfully old.'

'I don't think he's more than forty-five,' Marion retorted. 'It's those dark glasses that make him look so old.'

Tatave, who conducted his shadowing scientifically and very thoroughly, had the sense to ask the charwomen and old-age pensioners what they knew about the blind man. But nothing came of it. Nobody knew him and nobody could swear to having seen him in or around Louvigny before. Old Monkeynuts steered him out of Monsieur Théo's every morning and brought him back at night. At the end of a week he must have so grown to know the route that he did without his guide thereafter.

Berthe Gédéon and Mélie Babin shared Thursday's long watch, and their reports made it quite clear that the Phantom had two definite stands in the town. In the morning he played in the Place du Marché, in the afternoon on one of the 'islands' in the bus depot. As soon as Monkeynuts or Amédée appeared upon the scene he would move off. One or other of them would whisper in his ear his orders for the day, and then the Phantom would strike camp to begin a long musical tour which would sometimes take him to the outskirts of Louvigny.

Zidore set himself the task of finding out how much this strange street musician earned. On the blind man's behalf he boldly cut his Tuesday classes and followed him the whole afternoon so as to get a rough idea of his takings. It was immediately obvious that the Phantom was uncommonly altruistic and played beneath deaf or listening windows, on empty streets or busy pavements indifferently.

'Ninety-five francs for four hours' playing!' Zidore wound up morosely. 'Just enough to buy Nanar's food! And the dog wouldn't get very fat on that!'

Criquet Lariqué was entrusted with a very delicate mission. Marion gave him twenty francs in one-franc pieces and he had the task of attempting by all means in his power to get into conversation with the Phantom, while taking good care to space his contributions so as not to arouse his suspicions.

The coloured boy came back appalled and almost in tears.

'I gave him the lot,' he said bitterly. 'The lot! I was nice as I could be with him. Told him funny stories. Never a smile out of him. I've had the Phantom in a big way.'

They had to buy him an ice cream to console him for the failure of his mission.

'It's been a waste of money,' Gaby admitted. 'All we've found out is that the Phantom isn't very talkative. He must be made of stone not to laugh at Cricri's stories, they'd make a cat laugh!'

Marion confirmed what Fernand had noticed about the way the accordionist played. Wherever he took his stand, no matter how far away and unprofitable the site, the Phantom regularly and almost methodically played that haunting tune the girls liked best – *Pour deux sous d'amour.*

'And he puts more into that than any of the others,' Marion insisted. 'It's as though he was trying to make us get the tune on the brain. The kids in the Cité-Ferrand are whistling it all day long.'

'Musicians often get crazes like that,' said Berthe Gédéon. 'Don't you remember the one-eyed singer in the Faubourg-Bacchus: he had one sentimental song he used to sing twenty times an hour.'

'I'll say!' Zidore broke in. 'And it brought him in money all right. All the old girls in the district brought their purses out every time. That bloke used to make three hundred francs an hour with his *Nuit de Chine, nuit câline* ... Just think of it.'

They could usefully have investigated the question of the blind man's repertory. Marion felt that it alone far outweighed in importance all the oddities of his appearance. But that day their discussions went no further.

Every day, without fail, Fernand produced his streetplan of Louvigny and in red pencil traced on it the route taken by the blind man. As day by day he abstracted the information set down in Gaby's laundry book, he noted something that left the others flabbergasted when he told them of it. Apart from the two fixed points he occupied for about four hours morning and evening, the Phantom slowly and patiently explored the streets of Louvigny, never going in the same direction two days running, and always taking great care never to go down the same street twice, even if his last visit to it had been profitable.

When they studied the operations map again at the end of the week, they saw that he had covered the area between the main road, the Rue de Paris and the blocks of flats in the Cité-Ferrand. Fernand was warmly congratulated on his powers of observation and everyone began to formulate the wildest theories as to just why the blind man was tapping his patient way through an unknown town.

Zidore as usual saw money at the bottom of it.

'Monsieur Théo isn't in this for fun,' he would say. 'He uses the blind man as a sort of walking radar set to locate the loot a rival gang has hidden in the district. No one takes a scrap of notice of a blind man, but I bet he has a sharp pair of ears and keeps them open.'

From then on the blind man continued to work in a

west-east direction, and soon he was seen in the alleys of the
Faubourg-Bacchus and of Petit-Louvigny. Patiently the
Ten stuck to his tracks in the hope of some sensational dis-
covery and there was considerable argument as to who
should have the honour of dogging his slow progress.
Tatave and Zidore were furious when the redoubtable
Monsieur Juste all too often curtailed their police activities.
He seemed to hand out two hours' detention for nothing at
all these days; but luckily the holidays would soon bring
them blessed release.

Juan took over permanent watch on Monsieur Bollaert's
garage and the buildings attached to it. One evening the
Phantom was prowling round the neighbourhood and the
sound of his accordion penetrated the Rue César-Santini.
The gipsy boy was playing right opposite the garage with
the son of the housekeeper from a neighbouring block of
flats. Neither the Pierce brothers nor even Monsieur Bollaert himself had, in their comings and goings, noticed the
swarthy urchin wrestling on the pavement.

But Juan missed nothing that was going on in the neighbourhood. From the day he came his photographic brain
had recorded every detail of Monsieur Bollaert's men,
every single thing they did and each one of the lively con-
ferences that went on in the shadowy depths of the great
garage. Yet despite his vigilance he had been unable to discover the slightest clue as to their interest in the Phantom.

When the gipsy heard the accordion at the cross-roads,
he told himself something was bound to happen. For a
week he had awaited the blind man's arrival, for a week the
street had remained obstinately empty.

And now the blind man was there. Juan saw him reach
the bottom of the road and slowly walk towards the garage. At his heels trotted the noble Nanar, the tin cup in his
mouth. A lead was no longer needed, for the dog protected

his master with a touching devotion. When he was almost
level with the garage the Phantom must have found the sun
too strong for him, for he raised the white stick and carefully crossed the road to face the windows and exits of
Monsieur Bollaert's premises.

He opened his camp-stool, set it against the wall between
two doorways, unhitched his instrument, and deliberately
settled himself for his usual concert. Already a dozen small
boys had collected around him. Juan followed them, but
he kept one careful eye on what was happening opposite.

Paul Pierce had just returned at the wheel of his red lorry.
For the moment he was still inside the garage, tinkering
with the engine, half swallowed under the yawning bonnet. The first note of the accordion brought him jumping
down to the ground. He stared wildly out into the street,
saw the blind man installed on the opposite pavement, and
dashed for the office door.

Two seconds later, like a Jack-in-the-box, up popped
Monsieur Bollaert's pasty face at a dusty storeroom win-
dow and soon Paul Pierce's long red one appeared beside it.
The two men watched the blind man for some time and
Juan had every opportunity to study their strained ex-
pressions.

Just then half a dozen housewives came round the corner
and Juan suddenly saw Bonbon, the duty tracker of the
evening, prancing along behind them. He passed him without so much as a nod and went to ground fifty yards away
at the cross-roads. Every two minutes his fair head popped
out from behind the wall, took in the Phantom and his
audience and vanished again.

There was a movement in Monsieur Bollaert's. The two
Jacks-in-the-box had left their window, and Paul Pierce had
just closed the garage, but so softly that the rattle of the steel
shutter had barely risen above the sound of the accordion.

ATERIE

A new character was coming on to the scene, and Juan stared at the figure approaching along the Rue César-Santini. He had seen this gorilla of a man in a striped seaman's sweatshirt and a long-peaked blue cap somewhere before. He had just caught a glimpse of him in the Rue des Estaffiers, from Observation Post No. 3, the day he had been waiting to shadow Monsieur Théo. That evening the man had been taking a big, black dog, which could well have been Nanar, for a walk. It all held together. A moment's thought was enough to establish the connexion between the tough-looking characters from Monsieur Théo's establishment and the blind man.

Juan waited. The Phantom had ended his recital. He folded up his camp-stool, transferred the takings, a handful of small change, to his pocket and went off down the street. The man in the cap had now strolled level with the garage, pretending to read a paper. Juan let him pass and watched to see in which way he would go. At that very moment the Phantom had reached the next intersection and was about to cross.

Bonbon had stuck to his post. He saw the blind man was coming his way so he gave him a thirty-yard start before he followed in his track. The man in the cap kept straight on, too, and Juan realized at once that he was shadowing the Phantom as well. He felt his heart beat faster – Bonbon was, all unknowing, caught between the blind man and the man in the cap and there was no saying when he would give the game away!

Juan at once left his observation post in front of the garage and tailed behind to lend a hand to the baby of the Gang, should he get into difficulties. Thus, in this order, there was the blind man, unaware, or pretending to be, of all around him, Nanar, trotting at his heels, Bonbon painstakingly tracking the blind man and his dog, the man in the cap keeping an eye on the blind man over Bonbon's head, and, bringing up the rear, Juan himself watching them all and, despite his anxiety, appreciating the full humour of the situation.

As he walked along the gipsy could not but admire the clever way in which Bonbon played his part. He behaved exactly like a small truant who should have been home hours before. As far as he was concerned, the blind man did not seem to exist. He played hop-scotch along the pavement, singing to himself, scored innumerable goals with convenient stones, stopped to yell insults at other urchins of his own age, and then ran away before they could catch him, yet never for a moment lost sight of the

Phantom who was slowly making his way through the sun-bright alleys of Petit-Louvigny.

Confidently the man in the blue cap trailed after them without once bothering to look behind him. He stopped when he saw the blind man set up his camp-stool on the corner of the Rue de l'Aubépine and the Rue du Chemin-de-fer. To lull suspicion Bonbon carried on until he found a convenient doorway, into which he scuttled like a mouse down its hole. Juan laughed to himself.

The blind man went straight into a medley of old-time waltzes and popular songs, gathering a few wide-eyed small boys, a couple of dreamy older girls and the tramp, Spare-a-copper, who happened to be passing.

The man in the cap lit the butt of a cigar and took a careful look around him. However, he paid not the slightest notice to Juan who with dragging footsteps strolled along fifty yards away. From a distance he examined the audience round the blind man and then he hurried away up a neighbouring alley. Juan left the blind man to Bonbon, and cautiously followed him, for he thought this might be the more promising quarry. And yet nothing happened. The man merely ran his eye over the mean little houses at the roadside and their yards and gardens, giving on to the open country a little beyond Petit-Louvigny. They went from one alley to the next until they were back where they started, the corner on which the Phantom was playing.

Bonbon had just come out of cover and with fiendish glee was slowly walking round the tramp, stationary in front of the blind man.

'What about the Cadillac?' he asked quietly. 'Still won't go?'

The tramp shuddered and rolled his bloodshot eyes as he glared at Bonbon.

'Cough up,' Bonbon told Spare-a-copper and pointed at the blind man's empty tin. 'Or I'll go to the station shouting that you've got a couple of millions tucked away in your mattress. You stingy old miser! You just wait, I'll give you Cadillacs!'

Spare-a-copper did not cough up. He had just drunk his last few francs in the poky bar in the Rue de l'Aubépine. Bonbon's attack was too much for him and, turning round abruptly, he made off as though the Devil himself were after him.

Bonbon turned to see the big man in the blue cap come out of an alley with Juan close behind him. The latter waved an anxious hand at him and Bonbon caught on at once. He mingled with the children under the spell of the accordion. The Phantom had started to play *Pour deux sous d'amour* and the haunting refrain filled the empty Faubourg, golden with the setting sun.

The big man had taken up his stand on the pavement. But all the while he folded and unfolded his newspaper his eyes switched to the windows overlooking the corner and to the doorways holding the occasional listener. When the tune was over, one or two coins clattered into the tin. One of the girls even gave fifty francs.

Clumsily thrown, the coin rang on the pavement and rolled towards a drain. But the blind man leaned sharply forward and caught it with one sure sweep of his hand. All this was done in the fraction of a second, and no one in the audience was quick enough to notice it or to be surprised at so unexpected a reaction. No one, that is, except Juan, who was watching from the other side of the road and who happened to be looking in the right direction.

At first he was rigid with amazement. Then he signed to Bonbon and they both went back to the Rue du Remblai by different routes. Juan looked over his shoulder frequently, for he was badly scared. But no one followed him. The blind man, his day's work over, had started back for the Rue des Estaffiers, the big man in the blue cap trailing well behind him.

Gaby had treated himself to an hour's spying on Monsieur Théo's house, and now, on the last bend of the Rue Tournante, as he was making for the Impasse des Otages, he met the blind man. Housewives, children, railwaymen coming off duty thronged the busy street in their twos and threes, but the boy soon spotted the burly figure, crowned by a long-peaked blue cap, dogging the Phantom's footsteps. The man glanced uninterestedly at him and went on his way, peacefully chewing the butt of a cigar.

Gaby found the nine detectives sitting in a circle in the long grass of the cul-de-sac. For the last three days Zidore, Tatave, and Berthe Gédéon had been able to dispense with their bandages and Mélie Babin's face was as fresh and pretty as ever it had been.

'I must say the Gang looks a bit more presentable without its halt and maimed,' said Gaby, sitting in the middle of the ring.

They had been waiting for him before they discussed their successful day's work. Juan spoke first.

'I've got some news for you,' he said seriously. 'The blind man's being followed by someone else. Little Bonbon nearly got caught just now by a giant of a man who seems to stand guard over the Phantom. From now on we'll have to be very careful.'

'I know,' said Gaby. 'He's one of old man Théo's gorillas. We know of five as it is: the man who drives the newspaper van, Amédée, old Monkeynuts, and those two miseries Inspector Sinet plays cards with. The man in the cap makes six and there must be others as well.'

The news threw a gloom over the proceedings. It had been great fun to shadow the blind man in all security, but things would become much more difficult for the trackers if they had to reckon with this undefined threat in their rear.

'We'll make fresh arrangements,' said Gaby, who had noticed a look of patent alarm on the faces of the weaker spirits. 'If they give cover to the blind man, from now on we'll do our shadowing with the duty tracker plus exactly the same sort of cover ourselves. That's what Juan did this evening when he kept an eye on little Bonbon from behind the big fellow's back. It'll only make the game more fun and bring everyone into it.'

Much relieved, Tatave, Berthe Gédéon, and Criquet breathed again.

'There's something else,' Juan went on. 'I had a front-row seat for the Phantom's serenade in the Rue César-Santini. Bollaert and the two Pierce brothers were still working in the garage and the concert gave them a nasty shock. I may be wrong but from what I saw I'd say the blind man scares them stiff.'

'Why?' asked Gaby, his interest thoroughly aroused.

'First they watched the Phantom through the storeroom window as though he was a man-eating tiger prowling up and down outside, and then they bolted themselves in. They don't look as though they enjoy the music very much!'

'What happened next?' asked Marion.

'The man in the cap came right by me, but he didn't seem to take any notice of Monsieur Bollaert and his men. As I see it, the gang in the Rue des Estaffiers haven't the foggiest idea that there's something up between the garage people and the blind man. Maybe Monsieur Théo would give a lot to know that? We're further forward than he is in that direction.'

Gaby winked and pulled out his notebook: this was well worth going on record. Juan saved his most important item for the end. He stopped, stared unblinkingly at the others and then he dropped his bombshell.

'The blind man's only pretending to be blind!' he said with a broad grin. 'I watched him pick a fifty-franc piece off the pavement, smack! With a flick of the wrist, like catching a fly.'

There were cries of amazement.

'That's no proof,' said Marion. 'Blind people have a wonderful sense of hearing. The Phantom could have just put out his hand and simply caught it through sheer luck.'

'I was right,' Zidore shouted. 'A lazy policeman, the crooks from the Rue des Estaffiers, the gang of toughs in Bollaert's garage and now, on top of it all, a blind man who can see as well as anyone, who's probably the boss of the gang! What a collection! Searching high and low for hidden loot. It can't be anything else.'

Marion began to think he might be right, and so did Fernand.

'We mustn't accuse the Phantom until we're quite certain he is a crook,' she said, however. 'Tomorrow evening I'll keep an eye on him and I'll try to see what's behind those dark glasses. If I come back with the news that the blind man is really blind, will you believe me?'

'Of course we will,' Gaby answered. 'But don't forget what Juan's just told us; we've got to be more careful than ever, for we still don't know what's behind all this. Zidore and Fernand will.go with you, then.'

'No, I want to be on my own,' Marion answered obstinately. 'Your covering system could wreck it all either way; if the Phantom is pretending or if he has that sixth sense that gives blind men the power to know people are near them, even if they don't make the slightest sound.'

Gaby did not press her. He was sure Marion would succeed in her attempt.

Little Bonbon had completely lost interest in the blind man and his followers. A wild idea had been troubling him for quite a while.

'I'd like to know for sure,' he sighed, 'whether old Spare-a-copper really is a millionaire or not.'

The nine others promptly fell upon him and rolled him over and over in the long grass.

CHAPTER 8

Marion and the Blind Man

AFTER school next day Marion went straight home to put on her best dress. Madame Fabert was surprised at this beautification.

'What are you dressing up for?'

'I've a date with the blind man,' Marion answered, pinning on the brooch Fernand had given her.

This harmless vanity made her mother smile. It was just like Marion never to do anything by halves. Madame Fabert said nothing, for she trusted Marion. This independent little girl always went her own way, but she never caused the least worry or pain to her mother.

Marion gave her hair a final brush and then shut Fifi in the garden. He was too demonstrative and might well hinder her in what she had to do. Then she hurried away up the Rue des Petits-Pauvres.

Gaby and his detectives had been waiting for her in the Place du Marché for the last fifteen minutes. Zidore and Juan had gone off to pick up the trail and both soon returned with the news that the blind man had, for the first time, crossed the main road and was playing in the avenues of the Quartier-Neuf.

The Phantom had by now methodically explored half the town and it was the first time that he had entered the smart district which lay between the main road and Louvigny-Cambrouse.

Marion was off in a flash, while the others scattered to their posts to watch the Rue Tournante and Monsieur

Bollaert's garage. There had been a heavy rainstorm during the night and today the sky seemed bluer and the gardens greener. Marion felt delightfully out of her element when she reached the fine houses with their flowery gardens beyond the poplar-lined main road. She was able to track the blind man down by the plaintive notes of his distant accordion, carried to her in snatches by the gusty wind.

The Phantom was playing at the end of a broad cul-de-sac, in the shadow of a fine plane tree against which he sat. His audience was scanty – a few little maidservants at the windows, a housekeeper outside her door, and three small boys only too glad of this godsend to dispel their boredom. Although there was no sign of the man in the blue cap, Marion preferred to keep her distance for the moment before trying to strike up an acquaintance with the blind man.

Nanar, alias Toby, had cocked his tufted ears when he saw the slim figure in dark blue gliding from tree to tree. He sat obediently beside the blind man, but his bushy tail began to wag harder and harder the nearer Marion came.

She stopped, looked the dog right in the eyes and raised a warning finger. Nanar tried at first to argue, waggling his ears, but he soon lay down flat on his belly at the Phantom's feet, his yellow eyes obstinately fixed on his old mistress.

The last notes of the gipsy song sank into the silence of the avenue. The housekeeper came and put her offering straight into the blind man's hand. The little boys disappeared.

Marion waited motionless. At last the Phantom got up, picked up his stool and made off towards the main road, his white stick tapping the edge of the pavement. He turned the corner and started down an empty road leading to the vacant lots of the Quartier-Neuf. Marion followed him.

Behind their hedges of privet or syringa, at regular

intervals stood the free-stone or pebble-dash of pretty little houses. The blind man stood and sniffed the air. The scent of the syringa in flower must have affected him, for he set his stool against a hedge, grunted something to Toby-Nanar, whom the presence of a cat was making restive, and broke into his everlasting medley with renewed vigour.

Marion quietly approached along the opposite pavement, and stood still, her arms hanging at her sides as she watched the strange couple with passionate intensity. There was nothing to show that the blind man, if blind he really was, had realized she was there.

Suddenly, a pretty, well-dressed woman came out of a nearby house. With her was a small four-year-old in check shirt and cowboy trousers. When they came level with the blind man, the woman automatically opened her purse, took a coin out and gave it to the small boy. Timidly the cowboy placed it in the tin, stretching so as to keep his distance from the terrifying Nanar whose yellow eyes seemed to be gobbling him up.

They went on their way. The blind man slowly turned his head as though his eyes went with them and all the while he played on. Meanwhile Marion waited in the sunshine, not moving so much as a finger-tip. Nanar did not stir as he lay with his head between his forepaws in the shadow of the blind man.

The Phantom ended his short, non-stop selection. He paused as usual and listened to the murmur of the neighbourhood. Only the ceaseless stream of traffic along the main road passed the end of the empty street. Still Marion made no move.

The blind man had picked up his accordion once more. He began to play his favourite tune with a depth of feeling which tugged harder at the heart-strings than ever before. Marion felt a lump in her throat. The throbbing air of the gipsy love song spent its enchantment despairingly on an empty landscape from which the very birds seemed to have flown. The last notes fell away into the silence around them.

Suddenly the blind man seemed very tired by his month-long, patient pilgrimage through the unknown town. There was a world of weariness in the way his right hand lifted to his face and slowly removed the dark glasses.

Marion was overwhelmed. For several seconds she was able to gaze at the face thus plainly revealed, the empty pits that once had been his eyes, the bristly eyebrows and the purple scar that ran from one side of his face to the other beneath them. The blind man's eyes really were sightless.

Marion should have left it at that, but a curiosity as strong as her compassion held her to the pavement. Twice the blind man sighed, and wiped his hand across his face as though to brush away his weariness. Then he replaced his dark glasses and sat quite still, his head half-supported by his shoulder. Marion raised her finger to warn Nanar not to fuss. Carefully she stepped into the road and tiptoed forward.

Still the blind man did not move. He seemed to be asleep. Marion tiptoed forward very slowly, never taking her eyes off the Phantom's lined face. Her last step brought her so close to the blind man that she could have touched his shoulder. She held her breath. Nanar had got up on his forepaws and looked at her as though he could not think what was going on. Then, very gradually, Marion stretched out her hand and passed it slowly to and fro before the dark glasses which masked those sightless eyes.

Still the Phantom did not move. Marion repeated her manoeuvre. Abruptly the blind man's left hand flashed out and caught her wrist in mid-air with a speed that left her gasping. She gave a little cry and tried to free herself, but he had a grip of iron and held her tightly.

'Why have you been hanging round me like this?' he asked in an unpleasant voice. 'I can't see, but for the last ten minutes I've known you were here.'

In her dismay, Marion hit on exactly the right thing to say.

'I ... I was listening to the accordion,' she stammered in her gentle voice. 'It's ... it's lovely. Please play *Pour deux sous d'amour* again ... for me.'

The blind man shivered and let go of her wrist.

'All right,' he said. 'I'll play whatever tune you like, but give me something.'

Marion felt embarrassed, for she had come out without a franc on her.

'I've given you your dog, as it is,' she said, as though to excuse herself. 'Haven't I, Nanar?'

Nanar's bushy tail wagged frenziedly. Her words had found their mark. Marion could see that clearly in the blind man's face, despite the masking dark glasses.

'I don't know the names of the tunes I play,' he said casually. 'Every now and then I pick one up and learn it by ear. What did you say it was, *Pour deux sous d'amour*?'

'Yes,' said Marion. 'I'll whistle it for you. It's the one I like the best, and you seem to, too: you play it twenty times a day.'

She pursed her lips and launched into the tune *con brio*. The blind man's face suddenly seemed to light up. He folded his arms on the top of his accordion and leaned forward as if to enjoy his own tune from the lips of this child of the streets. Marion entered into the spirit of the moment and, as she put heart and soul into her whistling, she could see the unfortunate man's expression soften for a moment.

'What's your name?' he asked suddenly.

She did not answer.

Nanar had pricked up his ears. A burly shadow fell across the group. Marion turned quickly. It was the tough in the seaman's sweatshirt and he did not look very pleased.

Marion tried to get away, but it was too late. He brought his huge fist down on the girl's slim neck and squeezed it cruelly. Marion struggled with all her might, kicking the bully's shins as hard as she could. Nanar showed his long, sharp teeth, and prepared to spring to her rescue. The man had to let go. With a negligent shove he sent her flying ten feet or so.

'Hop it!' he hissed between teeth that still gripped his cigar stub, 'and don't let me catch you interfering in our affairs again.'

Marion got up and rubbed her grazed knees. She was white as a sheet, and although she was not frightened she was beginning to shed her illusions. The intervention of this tough and his threat made her feel that perhaps Zidore was right. Sadly she looked at the blind man slumped forward on his camp-stool and then she walked away to the main road without a backward glance. Sacco watched her go and then he turned to the silent blind man.

'What was she talking to you about?' he asked suspiciously.

'Nothing,' the blind man grunted. 'Music. She's the girl who gave me the dog.'

Sacco's fears did not seem in the least appeased.

'Remember what old Théo told us?' he went on. 'In a job like ours one wrong word can give the whole game away. We should have gagged you, that would have stopped you blowing the gaff.'

The blind man shrugged resignedly.

'I've been looking for you,' Sacco added. 'We've got to go back right away. Théo'll tell you why.'

They went back the shortest way to Number 58 Rue des Estaffiers. Monsieur Théo himself let them in.

'There've been some kids nosing round our friend here,' Sacco told him at once. 'And they're always the same kids. Who's that girl that gave you Toby?'

'I didn't ask her name,' Monsieur Théo admitted irritably.

'You should have thought of that.'

'I think she lives over on the other side of the station,' Monsieur Théo added. 'They call her the girl with the dogs.'

'Well, she was trying to natter to our old music-maestro just now,' growled Sacco. 'We'd have done better to get the brute from a proper kennels. It would have cost us a bit, but that would have been that.'

Monsieur Théo turned to the blind man.

'I've just been to the police station,' he said, lowering his voice. 'That fool of an inspector still doesn't smell a rat, and quite unsuspectingly he gave me a clue we might find handy. Come inside! I'll tell you all about it when we're in the dormitory.'

Marion rejoined the others. They were waiting for her lying flat on their backs in the grass on the shady side of the Impasse.

'Well, is he or isn't he?' Zidore asked her in irritable tones.

The others began to giggle.

'He is,' Marion frowned. 'But he's very quick for a blind man. Better keep your distance.'

And then, very simply, she told them what had happened, including the annoying intervention of the man in the cap.

'Are you all right?' Fernand asked.

'I'm O.K.,' said Marion, who never made a fuss. 'I've seen worse.'

'To cut a long story short, he is blind, but he's a crook who's up to something pretty shady,' Zidore went on. He had this idea on the brain.

'I never said that,' Marion protested. 'He's just unfortunate, and there's nothing to show that the people who look after him really are up to dirty work.'

'You've only got to look at them to make your mind up,' said fat Tatave scornfully. 'Zidore's right. The Phantom is a common or garden crook. Going blind doesn't stop you being just as bad.'

'It's not his fault if his friends don't look very prepossessing,' Marion answered with a tremor in her voice. 'That's no guarantee, look at Monsieur Manceau. He looks like an angry cat, but he's one of the nicest people and he's Mayor of Louvigny, what's more!'

She made them laugh, but she did not soften their judgement.

Marion looked away angrily and began to cry silently, as she chewed the end of her handkerchief. She was sickened by the unjustified suspicions the blind man had aroused in some of the others. She, on the contrary, and although appearances were against him, returned to the view that the Phantom and Monsieur Théo's men were involved in something very different from a sordid money matter. The children naturally could not be expected to find out what it was all about straight away, even if they pored over the clues they had already collected.

'Marion is right,' Gaby said. 'We dramatize things too much, and yet it's so easy to be given completely the wrong idea by the way someone acts if you catch him unexpectedly. For instance, you see a shabby-looking character washing blood off his hands and his knife. The first fool who happens to spot him jumps to the conclusion he's cut some old woman's throat and runs off to warn every cop in the town. But all it is is the poor chap's just been skinning a rabbit for the family dinner, and the only question is whether or not he pinched the rabbit, isn't it, Zidore?'

Everyone laughed then, even Marion through her tears, even Zidore the rabbit thief. Gaby's breezy exterior hid a cool and crafty brain which seldom led him astray.

Marion was grateful for the way in which he had summed things up. Most of the children felt rather small. It had only needed a few joking remarks to work a complete change of view in the Gang and to foster an almost unconscious sympathy for the blind man and his bodyguards.

'Don't cry, then,' Gaby added and put his arm round Marion's shoulders. 'We're not going to hurt your blind man. What we've done so far may help him one of these days.'

'He's not *my* blind man,' said Marion, stressing the adjective. 'He's *our* blind man.'

She wished above all else to keep her friends interested in an adventure which might bring into play all the generosity of which they were capable.

Fernand, too, supported her.

'We must go on with the game,' he said. 'But we've got to forget that Monsieur Théo, the blind man and his friends could be crooks and that it would be one up for us if we exposed them. We don't sneak to the police, and they haven't hurt us. But if they are in trouble, it would be terrific if we could help them. Everybody has a different way of showing they're unhappy, and these toughs can have their troubles the same as anyone else. It's harder to discover, that's all!'

It was still not seven o'clock, so the whole gang decided to forget the blind man and his mysterious doings and go for a bathe in the sandpit at Villemarie.

Much later, when Marion was going home, she was upset to discover that she had lost the brooch Fernand had given her.

CHAPTER 9

A Dangerous Game

JUNE soon slipped by, and the fine weather made the days within the gloomy walls of the school in the Rue Piot almost unbearable. An epidemic madness rioted through the classrooms, leaving some of the children day-dreaming and filling others with the wildest follies. Tatave and Zidore organized long-distance may-bug flights among the older children, and their form room was filled with a ceaseless hum. Each morning they brought in bushels of the insects, which they hid in their desks. It nearly drove Monsieur Juste out of his mind and he spent his time storming through the class opening and shutting the windows, shouting, and dealing out punishments on all sides. Fortunately he forgot he had given them two minutes later, for the school year weighed as heavily upon him as it did upon his pupils.

Juan often brought a tame sparrow in his satchel. He had christened the bird Picolo, and it was so well trained that it seemed to obey him by telepathy. A well-aimed duster would chase him out of the window, but he would come back through another, perch cheeping on the blackboard, disdainfully drop his visiting card on Monsieur Juste's diagrams and then, when the hunt grew too hot, would slip like a minnow into the safety of his master's satchel.

Gaby's duty was to give out the books and to set out the equipment in the chemistry experiments, and he carried it out conscientiously, but behind the master's back he engaged in a small supplementary experiment of his own – into the relativity of time. Moving so quickly that it was almost impossible to follow his actions, he would open the clock, give the minute hand a calculated push forward – a good fifteen minutes – shut the clock and, under Monsieur Juste's nose, return to his desk looking as though butter would not melt in his mouth. Since the latter, in a fit of exhaustion, would dismiss them ten minutes early, they occasionally gained as much as half an hour over the afternoon, and that was a godsend when the Ten had to track down the Phantom miles away in Louvigny-Cambrouse.

The blind man continued to explore the town slowly. It became more and more difficult to follow his movements, because when he was not escorted by the man in the blue cap, then Monsieur Théo himself was there. Marion's bold move had aroused their suspicions. Hence Gaby had to be careful how he used his trackers. For close work he preferred Bonbon, Criquet, Berthe, and Mélie; as babies of the gang they were more likely to pass unnoticed. Thanks to them they were able to follow the Phantom through the outskirts of the town and to determine that he visited the loneliest lane. Gaby could not get over it.

'What on earth's he doing down there?' he asked when his spies delivered their reports. 'From what Bonbon's told me he's picked up a bare hundred francs in the last couple of days, and he could have got that in half an hour at the bus depot or on the Place du Marché. It's crazy! You'd think he enjoyed walking round just for the fun of it.'

Fernand unfolded his street plan, carefully smoothed it flat and marked in the route he had taken that day. Marion leaned over his shoulder to watch. It was an excellent system that gave them a very good idea of where the blind man would be going the next day, for he never covered the same ground twice.

Soon the Phantom was taken across the main road on old

Monkeynuts' arm to explore the alleys of the old town. The
only district then left untouched was to the south, bounded
by the melancholy waste-land of the Clos Pequeux. The
longest days of the year had come and the fine evenings
kept people out of doors. The blind man was well aware of
this and stayed out until eight or nine o'clock, playing his
songs and old-fashioned waltzes and setting the older girls
dancing on the pavements. His takings rose. Of the Ten,

Juan was the freest and the least bound by home; he there-
fore made it his business to continue the shadowing outside
their normal hours.

Suddenly one evening in the Joyes' home they heard the
accordion playing in the middle of the Impasse Aubertin.
Gaby leaped to the window, but he took good care not to
stick his head out. The man in the blue cap was hanging
around, cigar stub hanging from his underlip, one eye on
the blind man, the other peering into doorways open to the
cool of the evening.

Half an hour later the Phantom was serenading the Rue
du Malassis. Zidore watched him pass slowly, the patient
Nanar at his heels. It was dark by now and he slipped out
only to bump straight into Juan, strolling behind and whistling the opening bars of *Pour deux sous d'amour*.

'Follow the blind man,' he hissed. 'I'll look after the
big bloke. He's not far away.'

Zidore trailed the Phantom all along the Rue Cécile.

The blind man stopped outside Number 104, nearly on
the corner of the Rue des Petits-Pauvres, to give his final
concert. At the sound of the accordion Zidore was amused
to see the astonished faces of Tatave and Bonbon pop out
of the second-floor window.

He turned the corner and hurried off to the Douins'
house. They had just finished supper.

Fernand caught a glimpse of his friend through the window and beckoned him in.

'He's here,' said Zidore excitedly. 'It looks to me as
though this is the end of his explorations.'

'I suppose so,' said Fernand. 'Let's have a look at the
map.'

They helped Madame Douin clear the table. Monsieur
Douin was sitting in his chair, puffing his pipe, an ironic
gleam in his eye as he watched the two boys. He was highly

amused by this business of the blind man, for he saw nothing mysterious in his behaviour. However, he was curious to see what the Ten, and more particularly his own son, would get from a situation which they had apparently created from nothing.

Outside, there was the usual pause and then the blind man took up the haunting air which had hung about the streets of Louvigny for the past month.

There was a knock at the door. It was Marion.

'You can hear him from the other end of the street,' she said when she had kissed Madame Douin. 'It's funny to hear it so close to one's own home. It's as though he was playing for someone special. But who?'

Fernand was miles away, staring straight in front of him. He was beginning to have a glimmering of what it all meant. At any rate an ingenious explanation had flashed across his brain.

The street plan was spread out on the table. Fernand took his red pencil and drew a line from the main road into the Impasse Aubertin, along the Rue du Malassis, up the Rue Piot to the corner of the school and then straight down the Rue Cécile to the cross-roads from which it had set out a month before. At a glance it was possible to see the ground the blind man had covered since his arrival.

The inhabited area of Louvigny was covered by a sort of spider's web, which followed exactly the network of streets. The Phantom had visited every one, the narrowest alley, the remotest cul-de-sac, and even the oddly spiralling Rue Tournante, which cast its triple coil around Petit-Louvigny.

Monsieur Douin got up to look at the map over his son's head.

'Well,' he admitted in amazement. 'You certainly seem to have got something. It's very odd the way the poor chap carries on.'

The blind man still played, and because Fernand had heard the tune now harmonizing with the twilight so often, for the first time he began to realize its hidden meaning.

'Anyone who aims to live off what people'll give him would never act like this,' he said, resting his finger on the map. 'In a town there are good spots and bad spots, and the stupidest beggar would take very good care to avoid *them*. Now, we've seen the Phantom in the worst places in Louvigny.'

'All the same he had half-a-dozen toughs to guide him,' said Zidore.

'Where we went wrong was right at the start when we thought the blind man acted as a messenger or a sort of secret agent for those people,' Fernand went on. 'But if we accept the fact that, on the contrary, Monsieur Théo and his men are helping the Phantom, then it's as plain as plain! Look at the map and run your finger along the route he's covered up to now. The blind man has been really exploring this town for his own purposes.'

Zidore and Marion were carried away by his argument. It explained in part the activities of the Phantom, but it made them no less odd. Monsieur Douin, too, seemed impressed by his son's deductions.

'I see what you're getting at,' he said to Fernand. 'But your blind man must have some very good reason for exploring an ordinary town like this.'

'I think I know that too,' Fernand went on with a wave of his hand vaguely in the direction of the blind man at his post outside on the street corner. 'Just listen. Can't you hear anything?'

As though to underline the uselessness of his tour of the little town the blind man was obstinately repeating his favourite tune. Monsieur and Madame Douin, Marion and Zidore did not speak for a moment, they were all under the spell. Then Marion's eyes opened wide as she looked at Fernand. She, too, was beginning to understand.

'For the last five weeks,' Fernand said, 'the blind man has been playing that tune at least twenty times a day, and putting all he knows into it. The rest doesn't matter. The selection he plays every time he takes up a new stand is just for show, to get people around him, to make everyone in the district listen.'

'And then he goes into the tune we all know by heart,' said Marion. '*Pour deux sous d'amour.*'

Fernand nodded.

'People who just hear it once or twice near their homes, or at the corner of a street, think it's no different from any other tune. But we've followed the blind man from the start and it means a lot more to us. It's as though he never got tired of signalling from street to street to someone he didn't know how to find.'

'Yes,' said Marion. 'He must be looking for somebody in Louvigny.'

'He'd find him quicker and easier if he went to the Town Hall or put an advert in the paper,' Zidore objected. He still had his doubts.

'We can't be certain of that,' Marion answered. 'If the Phantom is looking for somebody in hiding, or kept in hiding, he has to go about it very carefully. He doesn't want to run any risk in making himself known, so he's adopted a method that involves no one else. His signal can be understood by one man, and by him alone.'

The last notes of the accordion died away in the distance. The children looked up. Monsieur Douin opened the door and leaned out to glance down the Rue des Petits-Pauvres.

'That's that,' said Marion. 'It's all over. The blind man's back where he started from. What'll happen now?'

'We'll find out tomorrow,' said Fernand. 'If he starts out

on his rounds again, it'll mean we were dead right and that nobody can have answered his signal yet.'

'Come and look,' whispered Monsieur Douin, stepping outside.

They went over to where he stood in the narrow front garden. The sun had set and although the sky was still a lovely luminous green, night had already fallen in this district, which was forever darkened by the smoke from the junction.

The blind man was slowly walking up from the corner, his accordion slung across his back, his dog at his heels. Nanar himself seemed to be exhausted by the over-long day and slunk along with drooping head. They passed along the pavement opposite the Douins' house. Twenty yards behind strolled a burly figure in a blue cap, hands in pockets, staring around him with what he seemed to hope would be taken for indifference.

Marion hid behind Monsieur Douin's back. The big man glanced at the others, but did not recognize them. Ten seconds later another burly figure came round the corner and it too slackened its pace. They had been expecting to see Juan – but this was James Pierce, who had for some time stood for the enemy in the affair. Fernand and Zidore breathed a sigh of relief. Juan had not blundered into this game of hide and seek. He had scented the intruder's presence. James Pierce was still in his driver's overalls and as he followed the trail he made no effort to conceal the anxiety in his face. He too glanced at Monsieur Douin's house, but as most people in the street were enjoying the cool of the evening in their doorways, he noticed nothing unusual in the attitude of the children leaning on the garden gate.

At last the gipsy boy hove into sight well behind him. He knew by heart the blind man's route and he had no reason to hurry. He laughed when he saw his friends standing there like spectators at a race-course.

'Call it a day!' Zidore called to him. 'The blind man won't play again this evening, and it'll be dark in half an hour.'

'It's the lorry driver I'm after just now,' Juan answered. 'It looks as though he's trying to find out where the Phantom lives. If he does happen to discover the house in the Rue des Estaffiers, then Monsieur Théo and his lot had better watch out. Things could brew up pretty quickly.'

'Have you had your supper?' Monsieur Douin asked him.

'Not yet,' Juan replied. 'But there's no hurry. There's always a bite of something for me at home.'

His slender shadow slipped away towards the station.

'This is no joke,' said Monsieur Douin, shaking his head, a bewildered look on his face. 'You'll find yourselves in trouble before you're much older.'

He was a trifle worried, having seen the two men pass on the trail of the blind man, but the children's curiosity was infectious and he was longing to know more.

'You're playing a dangerous game,' he told the trio. 'Suppose there's dirty work behind this as there was in that business of the Horse?'

'There can't be,' Fernand answered. 'If there really was something crooked, those men wouldn't have wasted five weeks steering a cripple round the town when he's so easy to shadow. Don't forget Nanar's transformation either. Monsieur Théo and his men wanted to dress up that pair, the blind man and his dog, to impress one particular person.'

'It must all be part of a scheme planned ages ago,' said Marion. 'Somebody in hiding in Louvigny waiting for a blind man in black, a black dog called Toby, and that gipsy love song everyone in town's been humming for days.'

Monsieur Douin did not argue. Zidore and Marion said good night and went their separate ways, while Fernand obediently followed his father indoors.

'I hope you'll know when to stop if this business does look like going too far,' Monsieur Douin grumbled. 'There's just one thing I'd like you to remember. You think you're fooling Monsieur Théo beautifully, don't you? But he's a man with a past. They say he's done a fifteen-year stretch in jail, and you don't get that for nothing!'

'That's what his neighbours in the Rue des Estaffiers say,' Fernand laughed. 'But it isn't true. Monsieur Théo has been in jail, but on the right side of the bars – he's a retired police captain! No wonder he can walk into the police station at Louvigny as he pleases.'

'Where did you get that from?' Monsieur Douin asked in surprise.

'Old Monsieur Gédéon told Berthe. Her grandfather knows everything about everybody in the district, so it can't be wrong.'

Monsieur Douin still seemed disposed to grumble.

'Don't you worry, dad,' Fernand ended. 'We aren't doing any harm and if any good comes out of it, it'll be thanks to us.'

'I know,' said Monsieur Douin. 'And don't forget that the one thing in life that really matters is the trouble we give ourselves in order to help other people.'

Fernand nodded. In this light the game took on a fresh and exciting aspect, particularly as it might almost have been invented for the gang who brought laughter to the Rue des Petits-Pauvres.

CHAPTER 10

The Trap is Set

As usual on Thursdays the Ten had met on their bench facing the Café Parisien in the Place du Marché. Fine weather had set in at the beginning of the week and each morning the summer sun seemed brighter.

'I followed James Pierce all the way along the Avenue du Général-Cahin,' Juan was saying. 'When I got to the corner of the Rue Tournante, what do you think I saw? He was coming back as hard as he could go. I went on to see what it was all about. At the cross-roads there was a man on each corner looking as though they'd been posted there to intercept any awkward customers. It was pretty dark by then, but I could see they were that skinny couple who lodge with Monsieur Théo. They stayed watching the end of the road for about five minutes, long enough, I suppose, for the blind man to get back to the house. Then one of them gave a little whistle and they walked off to the Rue des Estaffiers as easy as you like.'

Gaby noted it all down in his laundry book.

'Something did strike me, though,' the gipsy boy added. 'That couple must have come from the Junction. They were wearing overalls like the regular railwaymen. Now, does that mean they're working permanently there?'

'I'd noticed that too,' said Marion. 'They don't look such down-and-outs as they did at first.'

The suspicious Zidore shook his head and was all ready to protest, but the Chief Detective got in first.

'From now on,' said Gaby, 'our front line is going to be

the Rue César-Santini. Monsieur Bollaert and his men mustn't be able to take two steps without having one or other of us on their heels.'

'Well, I'd better get going right away,' the gipsy suggested. He always volunteered for the tricky assignments. 'But I'll need some help.'

'Good,' said Gaby. 'Take Criquet, Berthe, and Mélie. Position them along the Avenue du Général-Cahin. If the Bollaert crowd do happen to make a sortie towards the Rue des Estaffiers then we'll know what's going on.'

With conspiratorial looks the small fry went off in Juan's charge. Bonbon and the seniors stayed with Gaby. The latter was only half convinced by the sensational deductions Marion and Fernand had announced the night before.

'I agree with you,' he said, 'that it does explain the Phantom's persistence and his peculiar behaviour. But it does no more than explain, and if the blind man upsets all your theories by disappearing or playing somewhere else it gets us a heck of a long way, doesn't it?'

'I'm sure he'll start a second tour of the town,' said Marion. 'He may choose other places to play his accordion but he'll go over roughly the same ground. Let's wait.'

It was nearly ten and the sun beat down. The Place du Marché was its usual Thursday hubbub as a stream of people surged between the stalls set up since the early hours of the morning. The tramp Spare-a-copper was weaving his way hither and thither among the crowd, taking good care all the time to avoid meeting Vairon, the policeman on duty. Thursday was a golden day for him. Suddenly he swerved off towards the Café Parisien, saw the children on the bench and made a slight detour to touch these idlers for their contribution to the poor. Then he recognized Bonbon, pirouetted like a ballet-dancer and was into the Café in a flash. The children laughed.

'Here comes Monkeynuts!' Fernand suddenly announced.

The old man was coming slowly along the Rue de Paris, stopping to greet the stallholders of his acquaintance. He made for the station, passing in front of the silent children, and went into the Café Parisien.

'The other one won't be long now,' whispered Marion. 'He needs old Monkeynuts to show him the way to the Rue des Petits-Pauvres. You wait and see.'

They waited, keeping an eye on the various figures who every so often detached themselves from the crowd.

'Watch out!' said Tatave. 'Inspector Sinet's taking his constitutional on the square. Shall we shift?'

'Let him come if he likes,' grunted Gaby. 'What we do isn't any business of his. We'll show him a trick he hasn't seen before.'

Out of deference to the weather, Inspector Sinet had at least discarded his atrocious bottle-green trench-coat and was wearing a well-cut, dark brown suit.

'All dolled up, isn't he?' said Zidore. The appearance of the Inspector usually threw him into a filthy temper.

Inspector Sinet was casually strolling towards the Café Parisien when his hawk-like eyes spotted the motionless children. He paused and then, making a slight detour to approach them from behind, he came up, apparently hoping to catch them red-handed in some conspiracy.

It was a wasted effort. The six children no longer spoke to one another and seemed glued to the spot. The Inspector came round to the front of the bench and nearly fell over backwards. The faces of Gaby, Fernand, Tatave, Zidore, and Bonbon were frozen into expressions of the sheerest imbecility. Marion stared into space, squinting horribly. All Inspector Sinet's politest remarks elicited not the slightest response.

'Can't you find anything better to do on a Thursday?' exclaimed the irate Inspector. 'Why should I have such a crowd on my hands? I don't know what stops me clapping you all into the cells.'

The children knew and were hard pressed to stifle a guffaw. Sinet turned his back on them and made for the Café Parisien and his first game of 'belote'. As he went through the door he thought he could hear a gentle whinny from behind him. He was unmoved by the insult. Everyone whinnied when he went down the passage at the police station.

It was Zidore who had imitated the horse, but the whinny stuck in his throat. The mournful figure of the blind man had turned the corner of the avenue and was slowly coming across the Place du Marché in the morning sunshine. He had Nanar on a chain and was seemingly being led through the hurly-burly of the market.

Old Monkeynuts was watching through the windows of the café. He saw the blind man arrive and hurried out, his basket of peanuts on his arm. The two men halted just in front of the station for a muttered colloquy and then the Phantom put his hand on the old man's shoulder and let him lead him to the other end of the square. Gaby half turned to watch them vanish into the narrow mouth of the Rue des Petits-Pauvres. The others listened, their hearts thumping.

Minutes passed. At last the cracked notes of the accordion could just be heard above the hubbub of the square. Fernand turned to Marion.

'You see, we were right. He's started again in exactly the same place.'

'That shows the other one still hasn't answered,' said Marion thoughtfully. 'The first round was a failure.'

Gaby still could not quite believe them, but he looked half convinced.

'I'm going with young Bonbon to have a look,' he said, getting up. 'The rest of you stay here.'

He was back a few minutes later, alone, to tell them that the blind man's routine was unaltered. At the end of each selection he sent out the heart-throbbing signal which had already encircled the town – *Pour deux sous d'amour.*

'We'll have to help him find whoever he's looking for,' said Marion decisively. 'He'll never find them by just playing a tune on the accordion.'

'Why?' asked Gaby, amazed.

'That someone is probably shut in. He can hear the tune all right, but he can't get out and answer, "Here I am".'

Fernand's mind had moved in much the same direction, though he had not dared to express his thoughts openly, for they showed the part his friends were playing in a bad light. Gaby was unwilling to give his yea or nay. He was awaiting further proof which would enable them to act more usefully.

'Take over from Bonbon,' he told Tatave. 'And see he comes straight back and doesn't stop to play the fool on the way.'

But the morning's honours went to Juan, for he brought Gaby just what he lacked, the evidence which gave colour to the theory that this long game of hide-and-seek was really a man-hunt. Just before midday they saw him coming with Criquet and the two little girls, smiles on all their faces.

'I've got some news,' he said with a broad grin. 'For the last few days' – Gaby started writing in his notebook – 'Monsieur Bollaert has been leaving his office at about six in the evening, getting into his old Renault, driving off towards Petit-Louvigny and not coming back to the Rue César-Santini. Two nights running I've blistered my feet walking up and down till all hours outside the garage without a sniff of Bollaert. This morning I thought I'd clear it up. Last night I had a look at that overgrown garden on the corner of the Rue du Chemin-de-fer and the Rue César-Santini. It belonged to the Benitez house, the one that had a couple of bombs on it in the war and has been a heap of rubble ever since. Well, I got over the wall and fought my way through a sort of jungle. Whew! That garden is overgrown! Bushes that high! I skirted round the ruins and got to the end where there's a wall between it and the Bollaerts' place. As I was going along it I found a place where the blast had knocked a great hole in the wall. All they'd done was block it with about ten yards of wire netting so I'd a wonderful view of the back of the Bollaerts' house.'

'What did you see?' asked Gaby.

Instinctively Juan lowered his voice while the others crowded round him.

'Next to the road there's a little one-storey bungalow where the Pierce brothers and their families live. James' wife was hanging out the washing, but she didn't see me. Facing it is Monsieur Bollaert's house, a posh sort of a place with a lovely garden and kitchen-garden. Well, it's been empty for quite a while! All the windows are closed and the blinds down. The lawn hasn't been mown for ages. I was there a good half-hour watching and not a thing stirred in the house. Monsieur Bollaert must have run off somewhere else with his wife. I bet the blind man scared them away when he came …'

'If Monsieur Bollaert makes for Petit-Louvigny every evening he can't go very far,' Gaby cut in. 'The district's cut off to the north by the sheds and sidings of the Junction, so he could only really be heading for the Quartier-Neuf. But if that's so, why does he make such a long detour? He'd get there twice as fast if he took the Avenue Théodore-Branque. We'd better find out where he does live now.'

'It's all very well for you to say that,' grumbled Zidore. 'Don't forget he uses a car every night. It may only be a twenty-year-old Renault, but I'd like to see you keep up with it on your two flat feet.'

'Keep your hair on,' Gaby told him. 'I've got another way of catching him. All we've got to do is to post ourselves at intervals along his usual route. Each evening we'll move on a little farther in one direction or the other and if he's gone to ground in some hideout in Petit-Louvigny, we'll be bound to find him in the end. Let's have a look at the map, Fernand.'

Fernand spread out his street plan.

'Show us the way Monsieur Bollaert goes when he leaves the garage,' Gaby said to Juan.

'It's very simple,' the gipsy told him. 'He turns right straightaway into the Avenue du Général-Cahin and follows it across the Rue du Chemin-de-fer and the first bend in the Rue Tournante until he reaches the little Square Anselme. On the other side of the square the avenue becomes much narrower and changes its name to the Rue de l'Aubépine. The end of that street runs into the last bend of the Rue Tournante and so, when he reaches it, Monsieur Bollaert must turn either left or right, bringing him out on the Rue des Estaffiers, at one or other of the two observation posts we've been manning at different points for the last four or five weeks.'

Gaby bent over the map for a moment.

'Now this is how the Gang will go into action,' he said at last. 'Just before six, Juan will go to his usual place on the corner of the Rue César-Santini and the Avenue du Général-Cahin. He'll keep the garage under observation so that if Monsieur Bollaert happens to go the other way he can warn the next pair at once. They'll be Marion and Berthe and they'll mount guard a little farther up the avenue at the first intersection on the corners of the Rue du Chemin-de-fer. Tatave and Bonbon'll watch the next intersection, the Rue Tournante. There's no need to put anyone at the fork at the end of the Rue de l'Aubépine. Monsieur Bollaert has to turn right or left and that'll bring him out either at the end of the Rue des Estaffiers, our old Observation Post No. 3, manned by Zidore and Criquet, or at the crossroads near Number 58, our old No. 2 Post, manned by Fernand and Mélie. I'll patrol between posts while we wait for him to start. It doesn't look much on the map, but it covers over a mile of road down which Monsieur Bollaert can't move without our seeing him at once. If his new home is in Petit-Louvigny we're bound to know where it is by the end of the evening. One other thing: except for the start-line which Juan covers, every post will be held by two watchers and under no circumstances must both leave it at the same time. One or other of them must keep his crossing watched the whole time. If Monsieur Bollaert's car passes either of the last two posts, Zidore's or Fernand's, they'll take a note of the direction in which it goes and tomorrow night we'll do the same thing, but with the Rue des Estaffiers as our start-line.'

'But we're setting a real trap for the poor chap!' Fernand exclaimed somewhat anxiously.

'Yes,' said Gaby. 'Monsieur Bollaert'll only be able to escape through the bolt-holes you and Zidore are going to watch, so keep your eyes open.'

CHAPTER II

The Street They All Forgot

By the stroke of six they had all been at their places for at least ten minutes. The afternoon had been stiflingly hot but the houses began to cast their shadows along the Avenue du Général-Cahin, and the watchers, sitting on the pavement, were glad of the shade. From time to time Juan would leave the corner of the avenue for a brief reconnaissance of the Rue César-Santini.

One glance was enough to make sure that Monsieur Bollaert was still in his office sending his papers flying, bellowing down the telephone and harrying his drivers. At ten past six the last of the crimson lorries returned to its stable with James Pierce at the wheel. As the heavy lorry went under the archway it discharged a sickening cloud of black fumes. A little later down came the steel shutters with a thunderous crash. The old Renault was there, parked beside the kerb in the shade of the office-storeroom.

Juan hurried back to his post at the corner. He had only to turn his head to see Berthe Gédéon's green dress two hundred yards farther on at the end of his range of vision. Marion was pacing up and down at the cross-roads, throwing stones for Fifi.

Gaby's one fear was to see the Renault escape down one of the side streets, but from his post midway between the two intersections he was glad to see that Tatave and Bonbon went about their duties as conscientiously as the two girls. At that time of the evening traffic along the avenue was too slight to hinder the watchers, but towards half

past six the district would be flooded with people return-
ing from work. If things became complicated that could
seriously delay the runners, and Gaby grew more and more
impatient as he stared down the avenue.

Six-fifteen. Glancing into the Rue César-Santini, Juan
suddenly saw Monsieur Bollaert stride across the pavement
and go to the offside door of the car. The gipsy slipped
back to the avenue and waved both arms to warn Marion.
Monsieur Bollaert shifted into a comfortable position behind the steering wheel, switched on the engine and pressed
the self-starter. Nothing untoward occurred. The old Renault woke to life and obediently swung into the Avenue
du Général-Cahin. There had been no surprise. The hunt
was on.

As it slowly turned, the car passed quite close to Juan.
Monsieur Bollaert, pale, hot, and untidy, drove with tired
eyes fixed on the road before him. 'He's had it,' Juan said
to himself as he raced off to join the two girls farther up the
avenue.

The Renault slowed at the cross-roads and went straight
on towards the Rue Tournante. Gaby was waiting between
the two posts. He crossed the road in front of the car,
forcing Monsieur Bollaert to slow up once more, and
then raced after him to keep on his tracks for as long as he
could.

Farther on, Tatave and Bonbon were at their posts, each
one guarding a corner of the Rue Tournante. But Bonbon's mind was far away. Two minutes earlier he had seen
a familiar figure at the end of the avenue and the sight had
sent his thoughts happily wandering. Spare-a-copper, the
drunken tramp, was coming towards them levying his toll
on the passers-by. This meant that, when the Renault passed
them, Bonbon had his eyes on something else.

'Hi! You asleep?' fat Tatave shouted at his little brother.

'Monsieur Bollaert's Renault nearly squashed your toes flat!'

'All right!' said Bonbon as he watched the tail of the car disappear round the bend in the Rue de l'Aubépine. 'He's on the right road.'

But Gaby was there already, quite out of breath, with Juan, Marion, and Berthe trailing behind him.

'I'm off to the first check-point in the Rue des Estaffiers!' he panted at Tatave. 'The one at the end of the road where Zidore and Criquet are on watch. Marion and Juan can go down to the one at the other end. You two guard the crossroads and don't go away. Monsieur Bollaert could well turn on his tracks and then we'd lose him.'

And away Gaby tore to the end of the Rue de l'Aubépine. He took the left fork which brought him out among the end houses of the Rue des Estaffiers. Zidore and Criquet were there, sitting on a bench in a little square in attitudes that showed their lounging to be the merest pretence.

'Well?' called the breathless Gaby.

'Well what?' Zidore retorted. 'We're still waiting for Monsieur Bollaert. He doesn't seem to be in much of a hurry.'

'What?' bellowed Gaby. 'He left the garage less than five minutes ago. Haven't you seen anything?'

'Not a thing!' said Zidore. 'The only thing that's gone by since we've been here was a heavy lorry from the goodsyard, oh, and old Zigon and his handcart. The Renault could have got through lower down, but I'd be surprised if it has; you can see Fernand and Mélie from here and they don't seem to be worried.'

'Let's see,' said Gaby. Doubts about the way his wonderful system worked were beginning to assail him.

All three went down the Rue des Estaffiers to the intersection guarded by Fernand. The latter was peacefully chatting to Mélie, one eye on the Rue Tournante. Gaby came down upon them like a ton of bricks.

'Monsieur Bollaert's just got past under your noses while you've been fooling around!'

Fernand and Mélie gaped.

'There's been no sign of the Renault so far,' said Fernand, 'and we haven't seen anyone remotely resembling Monsieur Bollaert. He must have got through higher up.'

'That's just where we've come from,' replied Gaby, more and more dismayed. 'He must have parked somewhere. Let's get back to the Rue de l'Aubépine as quick as we can.'

They started back, searching yards, side turnings, and gateways. There was nothing. Only a few cars parked here and there. Gaby hurried faster but they still could not find the Renault.

When they reached the fork in the road they ran into Marion, Berthe, and Juan, eager for the latest news. Gaby started by accusing everyone and finished by surrendering to the evidence – once he had passed the last houses in the Avenue du Général-Cahin, Monsieur Bollaert, as if by magic, had vanished from sight.

'In any case he didn't turn back again,' said Marion. 'There were five of us waiting for him. He's somewhere between the Rue de l'Aubépine and the two posts on the Rue des Estaffiers.'

'Where's Tatave?' Gaby asked.

'He stayed at the cross-roads, like you told him to.'

'He may have seen something after we'd gone,' said Gaby. 'If he hasn't I don't know what we're going to do.'

Fat Tatave was still on guard at the cross-roads, jumping out of his skin every time he heard a car in the distance. He was alone. When he heard that Monsieur Bollaert had

vanished, car and all, two hundred yards from the intersection he was watching, he was completely thunderstruck.

'The Rue de l'Aubépine curves a bit to the left just beyond the little Square Anselme,' he explained. 'I lost sight
of the car after that.'

'We should have posted a watcher at the fork,' Marion
said to Gaby. 'Then we'd have had Monsieur Bollaert in
sight the whole time.'

'I can't think of everything!' Gaby retorted angrily.
'Where's Bonbon?'

'He went the same way as you did,' said Tatave. 'A
couple of minutes or so after you'd gone.'

They looked at one another, appalled.

'But we should have met him on our way back,' Gaby
cried, in desperation. 'Now Bonbon's vanished … that
really puts the lid on it!'

In a body, they ran back to the square. Beyond it lay the
narrow Rue de l'Aubépine. There was no sign of Bonbon.
Gaby raced on ahead and as he rounded the bend he slowed
down and breathed a sigh of relief.

'There he is!' he called and turned to the others.

The solitary figure of Bonbon stood out in the sunshine
at the fork in the road. He was peering round, a puzzled
look on his face, and the arrival of his friends left him unmoved.

'Where have you been?' asked Gaby severely, seizing
his arm.

'I saw Spare-a-copper go by and I followed him to see
where he was going,' Bonbon announced calmly. 'That
tramp's my pigeon.'

'You and your tramp are beginning to get on my
nerves!' Gaby shouted. 'While we were chasing Monsieur
Bollaert like mad you were wasting your time hovering
round that old drunk! If we've lost his trail it's your fault!'

'Maybe,' Bonbon answered evenly. 'Anyway I've found where that old miser hides. He's fixed himself up very comfortably in the attic of an empty shed. And he doesn't do himself badly. He's got his Cadillac parked right underneath in a little wooden garage.'

Gaby went quite red and the others howled with laughter in the background.

'His Cadillac?' he snarled.

'That's right,' said Bonbon. 'Of course it isn't the latest model but it's not a bad-sized bus and I bet it would do seventy-five as well as the next.'

'Where is this shed?' Gaby asked him, his expression altering.

'In the other road,' said Bonbon, and he waved a vague hand towards the fork.

'Which road?' Gaby persisted. 'The one to the right, or the one to the left?'

'The one in the middle,' Bonbon replied coldly. 'You can't see it from here, it's hidden behind a sort of wall. Come on, I'll show you.'

Gaby and the others followed as, proudly, the baby of the gang led the way. Nobody dreamed of laughing now.

At the fork, in line with the Rue de l'Aubépine, two massive stone pillars had been erected a little behind and forming a sort of gateway to a row of houses on either side. The opening was screened from the gaze of passers-by by two small concrete walls, one set slightly behind the other. The chicane so formed could be negotiated by a car, and the whole recalled the check-points set up by the Germans at the entrances to their depots during the Occupation.

'My road's behind that,' Bonbon announced.

They went through the chicane and came out in a cul-de-sac, its far end close by the back of a three-storey house which must have been in the Rue des Estaffiers. All the right-hand side was occupied by the brick wall of a warehouse, but to the left there were four houses, each set in its own garden, whose flowers scented the silent street.

Marion looked around and noticed a rusty nameplate hanging on a nearby wall.

'Rue du Bout de l'An!' she called. 'It's the old name for the Rue de l'Aubépine.'

The children's eyes opened wide.

'I see it all now,' Gaby said at last. 'Before the war the Rue du Bout de l'An stretched on both sides of the fork. The Germans must have blocked this end of it when they commandeered the goods-yards. After the war was over, so few people lived in this bit of the road that they left it as it was. There are these sort of dead ends in nearly every town. They stay forgotten for ten or twenty years and then one fine day along come the demolition men and knock down two or three houses. Then up goes a factory or a block of shops and the street comes back to life again.'

'Come on!' Bonbon muttered impatiently. 'There's Spare-a-copper's palace.'

He pointed to a windowless wooden shed halfway down the road at the end of the garden attached to the nearest house. It was only a garage and belonged, apparently, to the house. The double doors were closed, but the skylight in the roof was open and a dilapidated flight of steps, with two or three treads missing, led up the outer wall to the attic above.

'A real tramp's castle!' Gaby muttered.

'The Cadillac's in there.' Bonbon pointed to the garage doors. 'Honest! Old Spare-a-copper does himself well.'

Gaby pushed the door open and peered inside. He shot out as though someone had thrown a bucket of cold water in his face.

'It's Monsieur Bollaert's Renault!' he said in bewilderment.

The boys elbowed one another as they pressed around the door to make sure it really was the fabulous eight-cylinder machine.

'That's it all right!' laughed Juan. 'There's not another wreck like it in Louvigny!'

'Shut up!' hissed Marion. 'If the car's there, the driver can't be far away.'

Silently, in single file, they squeezed their way along the wall to the garden gate. It was a lovely garden with a fine chestnut in the middle of a smooth lawn, well-weeded paths and beds of peonies in full bloom. Right at the end was a grey stone house half hidden behind privet hedge.

The french windows were open and so were the windows on the first floor. An elderly woman was sitting knitting in a cane chair in the shade of a chestnut tree.

'That's Madame Bollaert,' Juan whispered. 'I've seen her once or twice at the garage.'

'Keep out of sight,' Marion told the younger ones who were pressing against the garden gate. 'Now we know where Monsieur Bollaert lives. That's enough. Let's go.'

The garden was unexpectedly peaceful. You could not hear the noises of the town at all, and the whistle of the express trains hurtling top-speed through the junction only if you listened really hard. In spite of themselves the children were affected by the atmosphere of gentleness and peace which was distilled by this green retreat. Could Monsieur Bollaert be as guilty as his strange behaviour since the appearance of the blind man led them to suppose? Could a bad man live in a place like that?

Gaby was completely at a loss.

'Just what did we come looking for here?' he asked the others in perplexity.

They walked back in silence to the chicane for a final council of war. They had to make up their minds, and when in doubt it was always Marion who did that for them.

'I don't know what to think!' poor Gaby admitted. He looked questioningly at her. 'Shall we give up now?'

'No,' said Marion, in tones that did not brook argument. 'I'll go and see Monsieur Théo tomorrow morning and I'll tell him his blind man left one street out.'

CHAPTER 12

Marion in the Robbers' Den

MARION was very sorry not to have the brooch to set off her dark-blue dress. Before she went out, she slipped into the garden and cut a little white rose, hardly more than a bud, which she pinned on her dress in its place. Term had ended two days ago, so Gaby had suggested the strong escort of Zidore, Fernand, Tatave, Juan, and himself for her expedition. Marion, however, had refused it and she set off alone along the sunny streets with her little yellow dog gambolling beside her.

It was barely eight o'clock, and when she reached the Rue des Estaffiers it was practically empty for as far as the eye could see. She felt her heart beat faster as she neared Number 58. She listened. Not a sound came from the house and its shutters were still closed.

She rang a long peal on the bell. Monsieur Théo's room must have been right at the back of the house, for when the distant *brrr* broke the silence there was no sound of answering movement. Marion rang again, short, sharp peals this time. She heard a grumbling voice inside, and then steps approached the garden gate.

'Who's that?' Monsieur Théo grunted sleepily.

'Me, the girl with the dogs!' Marion answered. 'I've come to find out how Nanar's getting on.'

Silence. The man seemed to have completely forgotten the children who a month before had brought him the dog.

'Who's Nanar?' he asked, surprised.

Despite her anxiety, Marion was beginning to see the funny side of things.

'It's the particoloured mongrel I gave you for a disabled man,' she answered, laughing. 'That big dog you've had such fun dyeing black.'

In a flash, Monsieur Théo had wrenched the door half-open and stuck his bald head through the gap.

'So you did notice it after all?' he said, rather annoyed. 'And yet the dye didn't run a bit.'

'It wasn't me who recognized Nanar,' Marion said. 'The dog recognized me. They remember if you're kind to them.'

'Oh well, your Nanar is fit as a fiddle,' said Monsieur Théo. 'But he doesn't half eat a lot. He's costing me a small fortune.'

He cast a sharp but appreciative glance at Marion's pretty face, her blue dress and the little white rose.

'Good-bye!' he said in a rather surly voice. 'Don't come walking down here again, it's not the sort of place for you.'

And he shut the gate.

'I came to talk to you about the blind man too!' Marion called to stop him going away.

'What the blind man does is none of your business,' Monsieur Théo answered sharply from behind the door. 'Hop it!'

'Maybe, but I know something which I'm sure you don't and it concerns the blind man.'

Slowly Monsieur Théo reopened the door and looked in some bewilderment at the girl. The expression on his face was quite different. Marion forced a smile to keep down the alarm which was rising within her.

'What are you trying to tell me?' Monsieur Théo asked, lowering his voice.

Before replying, Marion glanced round. The street was

still empty and growing hotter in the blaze of the morning sun.

'My friends and I have found out that the blind man's looking for somebody in Louvigny,' she said. 'He is, isn't he?'

'That's true,' Monsieur Théo grudgingly admitted. 'Well?'

'We've also discovered that somebody in Louvigny is horribly scared of the blind man. Do you think it could be the same person?'

Monsieur Théo breathed in sharply and went very white. He opened the door wide.

'Come in!' he said. 'We'll be more comfortable discussing this inside.'

Marion hid a smile as she went in. She felt she had won already. She stared curiously at Monsieur Théo's estate, the big countrified-looking house, the beds of irises and pansies, the well-stocked kitchen garden and, in the background, that odd sort of barn, with its doors tight shut and the little barred windows which had so intrigued Zidore and Juan.

Monsieur Théo led her through the garden to a bench with its back to a hedge.

'Now!' he said bleakly. 'Tell me and don't give me any fairy stories. If you lie to me, you'll wish you'd never come here.'

Marion told him the whole story, from the very beginning, with all the little incidents that had made this new game so fascinating.

Monsieur Théo seemed quite put out to learn at the start that for over a month now he, his men, and the blind man had been watched and shadowed the whole time by mere children. As Marion was speaking, the barn door opened and out came Monsieur Théo's lodgers – big Sacco, cigar butt stuck to his lower lip, blue cap on the back of his head; the couple Juan had noticed; a little man with a rosy face, dressed like a tramp, and a tall, thin, skinny individual in railwaymen's brown denims.

They were all in the plot, for Monsieur Théo signed to them and they gathered round the bench to listen. Big Sacco looked at first as though he would explode when he saw Marion sitting next to one of the aristocrats of the Rue des Estaffiers.

He must have been Monsieur Théo's right-hand man, for Marion saw him take a notebook out of his pocket and rapidly scribble something in it when she came to mention the Bollaert Transport Company, its employees, and its owner. Monsieur Théo sat quite still as he listened to it all, leaning forward, the palms of his hands flat on his knees, staring sombrely at the barn door. Only his thick, bushy eyebrows twitched from time to time. When Marion had finished he said gravely:

'You've served us nobly. But for you the blind man might have searched the confounded town for ever and we should very likely have given the whole thing up. Can you keep a secret?'

'Yes,' said Marion. 'So long as it isn't anything bad you're going to tell me. I don't want to be mixed up in any dirty work.'

Monsieur Théo pretended to feel highly offended. The others burst out laughing. Even big Sacco seemed to find Marion amusing.

'Don't you worry, my dear!' Monsieur Théo told Marion. 'First of all I'm going to give you a bit of a shock by telling you just who the villains in this story really are. You and your friends are very sharp, I can see that, but all unknown to yourselves you've got things very wrong, because the ogre's not who you thought he was. It isn't big Sacco, it isn't either of those two suspicious characters be-

side you, and it isn't me, either, much as you suspected me
of hatching some dark plot and being a police spy into the
bargain! Nor, and pay attention to this, my dear, is it
Monsieur Bollaert, whom you mentioned just now as the
man we might be looking for. No, the real ogre in the
story, the only one, is over there!'

Monsieur Théo turned sharply and pointed to the barn.
Bewildered, Marion's eyes followed his finger. In the doorway stood a tall figure in black – the blind man. Slowly he
came out of the dormitory, fingering his dark glasses into
place. He came towards the bench, tapping on the gravel
walk with his white cane. Nanar on his chain gently guided
his master. Monsieur Théo signed to Marion to keep
still.

At once the blind man sensed the presence of the others
round the bench and the aura of hostile silence which surrounded them.

'I'm going up to the station,' he said dully. 'I'll be playing in the Cité-Ferrand this morning.'

Monsieur Théo made no attempt to keep him.

'That's right,' he said gently. 'You have your little stroll
round.'

On his way to the gate the blind man had to skirt the
bench and brush past the group around it. In so doing Nanar strained at his leash and furtively licked the hand Marion
stretched out to him. The men never said a word, but they
turned to watch the blind man. His mournful figure was
outlined in the gateway against the sun-drenched street.
Then the door closed gently behind him.

Marion turned to Monsieur Théo.

'The ogre?' she asked incredulously.

'One of these days I'll explain the things you still don't
understand,' he answered. 'But promise me you won't
say a word to your friends. One of them could wreck

everything by being just too anxious to help. First of all, have you any idea of the sort of place you've ventured into?'

'I can just about guess,' said Marion, staring at the men around her.

The others laughed and she blushed a little, although they were not laughing at her.

'You're in a sort of convalescent home,' Monsieur Théo explained proudly. 'There can't be many more in the world. I take in conditionally discharged prisoners who come out of jail quite destitute. I give them food and lodging and try to fix them up with temporary work so that they can adapt themselves honestly to everyday life. Yes, these rogues around us, including big Sacco, have all been inside to pay for their youthful errors!'

Marion's eyes opened wider as she stared at Monsieur Théo's lodgers.

She was agog to know why they had been to prison. Big Sacco was standing in front of her and watching her in embarrassment out of the corner of his eye. He guessed the question that was trembling on the tip of her tongue and, to the vast amusement of his companions, he blushed horribly. The others were more hardened and faced Marion's stare without faltering.

Monsieur Théo began to laugh.

'Go on, don't be afraid,' he told the girl. 'Make them confess their crimes one after the other if that sort of thing interests you. But don't imagine you'll hear any thrilling adventures. There are thousands of ways of going wrong and thousands of ways of getting caught, but when you come to look at it it's all a matter of stupidity. No man worthy of the name has the right to risk his freedom just for a bit of money to put in his pocket.'

Marion hesitated. They had all treated her so kindly that she did not want to betray the trust she saw mirrored in their eyes by awakening memories of things they would prefer to forget.

She smiled and lowered her head.

This pleased Monsieur Théo.

'Poverty and bad luck make more criminals than the desire for easy money,' he said emphatically. 'The trouble is that if you've got away with it once it's harder to resist the temptation the next time. So one crime leads to another and really hardened crooks end up by being quite unable to break out of the vicious circle. The best thing that can happen to petty thieves, who've been driven to crime because they're desperate or really down and out, is for them to be caught red-handed the first time. If they're decent people at heart, their punishment does them good and they don't come back again, but what really matters is that they should regain the urge to live simply and honestly.'

Marion did not dare utter a word.

'There are no old lags among these men,' Monsieur Théo went on, 'and you were right not to ask them for their stories. They've taken their punishment and they've squared their debt to society. Prison is just an unpleasant memory and they've given up the idea of living off their neighbours for good and all.'

'That's the gospel truth,' said the little red-faced man in a husky voice. 'I feel as innocent as a new-born lamb. What about you, Lofty?'

'I'm as pure,' said that long streak of misery, 'as I was at my First Communion. Word of honour!'

Marion turned to the other two.

'We're just a couple of navvies,' said the first and swelled his muscles. 'Can you remember being up before the beak, Toto?'

'The beak?' said Toto angelically. 'What beak? All I know was they sent me off to a boarding-school in the country for five years and taught me to stitch mail-bags. It got a bit boring by the finish and nowadays I can hardly bear to walk past a post office.'

Big Sacco still stood there crimson-faced and tongue-tied. Monsieur Théo teased him gently.

'That chap,' he told Marion, 'spent three years as head cook in a jail. By the look of him his mates can't have had many of the best bits.'

Marion burst out laughing.

'So you see,' said Monsieur Théo, 'our hotel doesn't put up murderers. Only poor thieves down on their luck.'

'What about the blind man?' Marion asked.

'We're coming to him,' replied Monsieur Théo. 'You're dying to know all about him, but if I told you now it might stop you helping him as you have been doing. Why? Because he's got a lot more on his conscience. Will you trust me? As it happened, I had to spend fifteen years among the worst sorts of criminals. But even among those there were men who were worth helping, men who deserved to get back into honest society. I'm not joking! I was in a pretty good position to weigh up the good and evil in them. Remember this, my dear, Justice does not relent to those who are sorry for what they have done, and who have paid for their crimes. Is there any harm in doing something about this and treating men like that more leniently than the law itself? At first sight the blind man is one of the untouchables, the dregs of the criminal world, a dangerous animal whom people would be only too glad to see die. But he isn't a murderer, and he has paid the penalty, and so that's why I'm appealing to the kindness of your heart, my dear.'

Marion slowly nodded her agreement.

'Good,' said Monsieur Théo. 'You go back to your friends and don't worry. Tell them to wait in patience until this evening. In the course of the day Sacco and I will make some careful inquiries about this Monsieur Bollaert who's been sent running off to the other end of Louvigny at the sight of the blind man. At six o'clock you and your friends slip into this forgotten street where nobody goes. Wait there. Don't make a noise and don't show yourselves. A little later, when Monsieur Bollaert gets back to his hideout, the blind man will come to serenade him from the garden gate. That's the time for you to come into the open. A lot of children round him will take away from the horror that still clings to his name. Is that a promise?'

'We'll be there at six o'clock,' said Marion as she rose to her feet. 'All ten of us.'

She whistled to Fifi and walked lightly away towards the gate without a backward glance.

As Monsieur Théo's thieves watched her go they felt some shame, but much more regret. Between them they could muster a good number of years in prison, and having just had Marion there made them realize for the first time how wasted those years had been.

Five minutes after she had left, a little news van pulled up outside Number 58 with a squeal of brakes. Rat, the driver, jumped out on to the pavement, followed by Amédée, the newspaper seller from the bus depot. Sacco let them in.

'We came to see if you'd anything for us on our way to work,' Rat told Monsieur Théo.

'There's nothing for this morning,' said the ex-policeman. 'Anatole's giving his concert in the Cité-Ferrand. But we've got a slight change of plan this afternoon.'

He then explained to them the decisive turn the blind man's affairs had taken, thanks to the children. Popaul, Lofty, and the other two were about to go off to the goods-yards. They joined the rest and lingered to hear their benefactor's last-minute instructions.

'We'll leave it to the children,' said Monsieur Théo. 'They'll get on all right without us. Rat, you'll go and have a look at this street right away with Amédée. Tell Monkey-nuts, and he can guide the blind man there at zero hour. Take care, though and don't alarm the neighbours!'

CHAPTER 13

The Boy in the Garden

IT was six o'clock and the afternoon was drawing to a close. The sun was low enough in the sky to lengthen the shadows of the trees with the promise of the cool of evening. After one mad dash had carried them to the end of the forgotten street, the children enjoyed the refreshing scent of the neighbouring gardens. They were hidden at the end of the cul-de-sac under the down-swept leaves of a chestnut tree whose branches overhung the broken wall of the last garden.

'That's all I know, and that's all I can tell you,' Marion had to tell them every two seconds. 'We've just got to wait. The blind man's sure to come.'

The sleepy street was empty. The sky was blue, with a slight golden haze.

A quarter of an hour later came the sound of a car slowing down to negotiate the chicane across the other end of the road. The Ten watched Monsieur Bollaert's decrepit Renault heave into sight. With an ear-splitting screech of its brakes it pulled up in front of the garage, its nearside wheels half on the pavement.

More pale and worried than ever, Monsieur Bollaert got out to open the doors wide. As he put his car away it backfired explosively. Then he came out and stood still on the pavement for a moment listening, as though in the silence he could hear the collective heartbeat of the watching children.

'He looks as though he's worried about something,' Marion whispered to Fernand.

Monsieur Bollaert stared hard at the end of the cul-de-sac, but the chestnut hid its spies too well and he saw nothing. Carelessly he kicked the garage door shut.

There was no movement in the garden which surrounded the grey-roofed house behind its flowering privet. He walked towards the gate, drawing his key-ring from his pocket, opened it, and, after one final glance over his shoulder, vanished from sight.

Barely two minutes later a ragged figure appeared in the mouth of the chicane. Spare-a-copper! The younger children began to snigger.

'He knows the routine of the house,' murmured Gaby, cuffing Bonbon and Mélie to restrain their ill-timed giggles.

The tramp slunk into the forgotten street with as much caution as the children.

Finding that the road was as quiet and unpeopled as usual, he picked up the stub of the cigarette Monsieur Bollaert had just thrown away and drew in a few luxurious lungfuls of smoke. Then he crept towards the garage and peered through the door. The car was inside all right. Reassured, Spare-a-copper heaved himself up the creaking staircase and plunged into the attic, safely home.

'That clumsy old scarecrow is going to wreck everything at the critical moment, if we're not careful,' whispered Fernand.

'He'll take care to lie low,' said Gaby. 'The old soak doesn't need our secrets or Monsieur Bollaert's.'

The small fry grew more and more excited and began to twitter in the shadows like birds in a nest.

Marion sharply silenced them by shaking her finger. Above the muffled sound of the streets nearby a scarcely audible thread of music emerged.

'It's him,' she whispered. 'Keep still.'

The blind man must have been walking very slowly

towards the head of the forgotten street playing his favourite tune – *Pour deux sous d'amour!* There was something grippingly pathetic about the plaintive melody which swelled above the murmur of the town and grew louder the closer the player approached the cul-de-sac. Marion felt her heart contract. She alone half understood the tearful message of the old gipsy love song and half guessed the part this lonely backwater would play.

Softly the Phantom stole round the edge of the chicane. Nanar was well trained and guided his master to the pavement.

'Come on!' Marion told her friends. 'He's all ours now!'

One by one they came from the shadows. The blind man had been warned, and he seemed almost to expect the sound of their footsteps. Marion halted them by the garden gate. The softer light of evening gilded the still leaves and the roof of the grey house. The french windows and the bedroom windows were open to the cool. Madame Bollaert's chair was under the chestnut tree, but there was not a soul in sight.

'We're all here,' said Marion in her gentlest voice. 'You've found the right spot.'

The blind man nodded, but did not speak, as all the while he manipulated his aged instrument. Of his own accord he had stopped and turned to face the garden. Then he began to play a little more loudly in the midst of the listening children. The old gipsy love song they had so often heard now sped out into the empty garden with a new bite to it, smooth and compelling, silencing all the birds in the vicinity.

Fernand was the first to spot the slight movement in the shrubbery. A gentle nudge warned Marion.

Furtively a slender figure was gliding from bush to bush,

now full in the sunlight, now half lost in the shade of the trees. For minutes it vanished and then the breathless children saw it standing on the gravel path which led to the gate.

With eyes wide in astonishment, a little boy of about ten came timidly towards them, towards the blind man and his dog, towards the bewitching music which woke the echoes in the forgotten street. He was pale and fair-haired and so slender in his spotless white shirt and shorts that he could have been mistaken for a girl.

A second later he was up against the gate, clutching it with both hands, his head protruding through the bars, as, wild-eyed, he stared at the odd little group formed by the blind man and the ten children.

The Phantom had heard his footsteps lightly crunch the gravel. Instinctively his head turned towards the little boy who faced him. The accordion played more softly, more bewitchingly.

Seconds passed and then the boy seemed suddenly to remember something. Both arms gently stretched between the bars towards the big black dog.

'Toby!' he called in a shaky voice.

Toby-Nanar never scorned any advance. He leapt over to the gate and let his head be gently stroked.

Abashed, the Ten watched what was going on without uttering a word or stirring a finger. The slightest sound, the smallest gesture could have broken the spell and put to flight the figure which seemed to have appeared by magic. Yet a tune on the accordion had been enough to raise from his concealment the person held hidden in the heart of Louvigny.

Marion, better informed than any of the others, could grasp what moved the boy imprisoned in the park. He certainly remembered the tune and thought he recalled the dog, but the blind man was still a complete stranger to him.

Suddenly he withdrew his arms from between the bars and stared hard at the musician's set face and the dark glasses that gave it such a faraway look. Marion saw his own cloud with sorrow and disappointment.

And then everything changed. They saw Monsieur Bollaert crash out of the house and rush madly towards the gate crying out for help. At the sound, his wife came round the corner of one of the paths. She saw in the distance the little boy at the gate, the dark figure of the blind man standing on the pavement, and she began to run after her husband.

Monsieur Bollaert reached the gate. Roughly he pulled the boy away and almost threw him into the arms of his wife who had come panting up behind. White-faced, Madame Bollaert hurried back to the house, dragging the child along.

He looked back now and again to the gate and his expression was heartbroken.

Monsieur Bollaert came closer.

'Go away!' he screamed in rage. 'Or I'll telephone for the police!'

The blind man had stopped playing, but he did not move. His face was still expressionless, but more pale.

'Send for the police,' Gaby calmly answered. 'This is a public road. Anyway, the blind man's got a proper licence from the Town Hall so no one can stop him earning his living. Why are you so scared of him?'

Monsieur Bollaert stared wildly at the children and then laughed uneasily.

'You little devils!' he growled. 'While you're at it why don't you join hands and dance round him? Five years ago he had his picture on the front page of every paper and there was a reward of ten million francs, dead or alive, on his head. What do you know about him? Not a thing! He's lulled you all to sleep with his accordion and you think it's great fun to follow him from street to street as though he were the gentlest and most inoffensive man in the world!'

One by one the children moved away leaving a void around the Phantom, until only Fernand and Marion were left beside him.

'He can't hurt anyone,' Marion smiled as she answered Monsieur Bollaert. 'He's blind. Why should we be frightened of him? Honestly, he's not going to eat us.'

As she said this she had turned to her friends. Gaby was the first to come back, then Zidore and Juan, followed a little later by the younger children, and lastly by fat Tatave, the coward-in-chief. They all seemed rather ashamed of having yielded to a moment's panic.

'I don't hold it against you,' Marion told them, 'but if

you hadn't come back, Fernand and I would have left the gang.'

Meanwhile Spare-a-copper's dirty, whiskery, red face had peered furtively out of the attic skylight to see what was going on. Noticing on one side of the gate the blind man and his flock of children, and on the other the master of the estate, he quickly withdrew it, but not so quickly that Marion's sharp eyes did not spot him.

For the last time Monsieur Bollaert stared hard at the blind man as though he wished to imprint on his mind every detail of what he saw.

'Now go away!' he told the children in a gentler voice. 'It'll be best for all concerned.'

Then he turned his back on the silent cluster and strode away to the grey house.

'Has the little boy gone?' the blind man whispered, almost inaudibly, to Marion.

'Madame Bollaert took him indoors,' she replied. 'It's all over for this evening, he won't come into the garden again.'

'Let's go,' said the blind man, fumbling for Nanar's leash.

The children stood aside to let him by. Gaby looked inquiringly at Marion.

'I'm staying behind with Fernand,' she told him. 'Take the others to the Impasse des Otages. We'll be with you in a minute or two.'

The sun went behind the clouds. The forgotten street was overcast. Rain seemed on the way. The children looked sulky and rebellious, but none dared oppose Marion.

She waited until she saw them disappear through the chicane and then she signed to Fernand. Both crept up the stairs outside the garage. The little attic door stood ajar, yawning darkness beyond. Fernand risked a peep into the tramp's hovel.

Spare-a-copper was sitting on a thick heap of rags that served him as a mattress. His tensed and threatening attitude was like that of an animal at bay in its lair.

'What the devil are you doing up here?' he growled throatily. 'Beat it! Or I'll knock you head first downstairs!'

'You at home?' said Marion with a mocking grin.

'Course I am. I'm the oldest tenant in the place,' the tramp retorted. 'Been here ten years and more in this rat's palace.'

'Like us to tell Monsieur Bollaert?' Marion went on undismayed.

At once the tramp became more amenable.

'Oh my dear eyes, what a dog's life I do lead,' he sighed. 'As if things weren't hard enough for me already. Leave me alone and keep quiet about this. What good would it do you to have me chucked out of here?'

'I was only joking,' said Marion. 'May we come in: we won't stay long.'

Spare-a-copper consented ungraciously. Marion and Fernand, one behind the other, entered the narrow, low-ceilinged hovel, littered with rags, junk, and old papers.

They both sat on the floor and faced the suspicious drunkard.

'If you've been here for the last ten years,' Marion began, 'you must have seen and heard quite a lot?'

'Not a thing!' Spare-a-copper retorted. 'It's the quietest place in Louvigny. No neighbours, no cops, no worries! Unfortunately, Monsieur Bollaert took it into his head to buy the place up and settle his family in. Since they've been here I've had to sleep with one eye open all the time. It's not that they're noisy or anything like that, it's just that I don't feel I can call the place my own now.'

'Ah?' said Marion, pricking up her ears.

'Yes,' the tramp went on complainingly. 'They came

here in the middle of the night about three weeks ago, with a great red lorry full of furniture, china, linen, the whole darned lot. There was Monsieur Bollaert and those two Englishmen from the garage, the Pierce brothers, and two other drivers. It took them till early morning to move in, and believe me those blokes didn't slack. I didn't dare move and I couldn't get a wink of sleep. Of course they thought they were by themselves, and as no one lives in this bit of road they talked at the top of their voices.'

'What were they talking about?' asked Fernand.

'Oh, this and that,' Spare-a-copper replied and winked. 'I'd been out on the booze and when I'm in that state things go in one ear and out the other.'

He stopped and glowered at his two visitors.

Marion saw in his eyes that he knew much more than he would say and also that he guessed what her next question would be.

'Who is the little boy in the garden?' she suddenly asked.

Silence fell. The old drunkard lowered his head to hide his face. It was hard for him to betray the secret which tortured one of his brethren in misfortune.

'He's the blind man's son,' he muttered.

CHAPTER 14

The Kidnapper

MARION and Fernand counted upon catching up with the blind man before he reached the second crossing in the Rue Tournante. He was not there. Nor was there the slightest sign of his dark, slow-moving figure in the stretch of the Rue des Estaffiers leading to the allotments in Petit-Louvigny. This struck Marion as odd.

'Where's he gone?' she said anxiously. 'He can't have reached Monsieur Théo's house.'

At once she connected this disappearance with what Spare-a-copper had just told them, and with the extraordinary scene in the forgotten road. The blind man had hardly said a word, but he had left with an ominous expression on his face and had gone into the town looking like a condemned man walking to the scaffold.

'The main road?' Fernand murmured.

The two children took one panic-stricken look at one another and realized at once. They raced off towards the Avenue du Quartier-Neuf. Away in the distance they could see the blind man pressing on ahead, straight across the Square Théodore-Branque, ignoring the traffic that brushed past him. He had dropped Nanar's lead and the frightened animal leaped around his master, seizing his sleeves in his teeth and trying to pull him back to the pavement.

It was about two hundred yards from the square to the main road, down which a stream of vehicles poured at full speed with an unbroken roar, and Marion and Fernand reached it at almost the same time as the blind man,

He had taken two steps into the dangerous roadway. One car had slammed on its brakes and swerved sharply to miss him. The children leaped forward, just in time to drag him from under the wheels of a heavy lorry and to pull him back on to the pavement.

The poor man shook in every limb.

'Home you come,' gasped Marion. 'Your friends are waiting for you.'

Obediently he let them take him. The worst seemed over. A small crowd had collected on the other side of the road and curiously watched the two children, who had been so quick to rescue a blind man who had ventured on to the perilous crossing, and who were now leading him away.

'Is he all right?' somebody called.

'Fine,' answered Marion, with a forced smile. 'We're just taking him home.'

Monsieur Théo was quick to let them in. He, too, had begun to feel seriously worried. Marion whispered to him what had happened, while the blind man and his dog escaped to the cool and silent haven of the dormitory.

'My friends and I'll try to get him to see sense,' said Monsieur Théo, making Marion and Fernand sit down on the bench in the shade of the hedge. 'As for the little boy, well, I always thought it would finish up like that. The ogre now knows that his son is being looked after by a decent family and that he lives in the neighbourhood near him. It should be worth a bit to him to have his mind at rest. He'll have to make do with that.'

'Ogre.' This was the second time Marion had heard Monsieur Théo use that ominous word. Now she wanted the whole truth.

Monsieur Théo looked from the boy to the girl, sitting one on either side of him.

'Don't broadcast what I'm going to tell you,' he said, his thick bushy eyebrows gathering in a frown. 'Nowadays the ogre of the fairy-stories goes under another name, though mothers and fathers don't find it any more pleasant. Do you know what it is?'

'I do,' said Fernand. 'It's a kidnapper. He's a filthy swine who steals other people's children and holds them to ransom.'

'Generally kidnappers come to a sticky end,' Monsieur Théo replied. 'The police don't use kid-gloves where people like that are concerned. Hunted like a mad dog, the man ends up by getting rid of his prisoner.'

Marion could not believe her ears.

'And the blind man's a kidnapper?'

'Well, let's say he was, some years ago before he went blind,' Monsieur Théo continued. 'You were too small then to have been able to read his name in the papers. Even today he has to take good care to keep it dark, people see red where kidnappers are concerned. All I can say is that at the finish he got caught like all the rest and that his career ended in a very stiff sentence. And this is where the story gets a little complicated.'

'He went blind in prison?' said Marion.

'We'll come to that. Astounding though it may seem, this man was married, he had a boy of his own and he led a family life like so many part-time crooks. In just retribution, the court which judged and sentenced him went a bit further – they deprived him of his rights as a father. He had taken away other people's children, his own was taken away from him. An eye for an eye and a tooth for a tooth! As the mother happened to die, the authorities took charge of his little boy. From his prison the father, through intermediaries, tried to find out what had happened to his son. But in cases of that sort, and especially when one of their orphans has been legally adopted, the authorities keep their secrets.'

'But however did he pick up the trail in Louvigny?' Fernand asked.

'I'm coming to that,' said Monsieur Théo. 'Do you know the rogue who's been driving the news van for the last two years, we call him Rat?'

'We spotted him right from the start,' Fernand answered. 'Every evening at about five he used to deliver his papers at the bus depot and at the same time pass a message to Amédeé and Monkeynuts. Soon afterwards the old chap would lead the blind man off in a fresh direction.'

'Well, in a way Rat was the start of the whole business. He shared a cell with our man for six months. When he'd served his sentence, he came to me, as so many others have done, and I managed to find him this job as a driver, which seems to have suited him well enough. Mark this, though, so far I'd had nothing to do with the kidnapper. Rat didn't even mention him to me, all the same he kept in touch with the ogre, and sent him parcels every now and then. Now what goes into a prisoner's parcel? Soap, sausages, cigarettes, books, weekly papers. Among them all one fine day our fellow put this copy of the *Louvigny Express*. Here, we'll see if your eyes are as sharp as the blind man's were then.'

From an inner pocket Monsieur Théo drew a sheet of newspaper. It was yellow with age, and he unfolded it carefully across his knees. Marion and Fernand leaned forward eagerly to see. The foot of the page was filled by a clear enough photograph of the official opening of Louvigny's new Town Hall, in the middle of the Grand-Rue. In the background were the new buildings, all gleaming white, the beflagged balcony and on it the Mayor, Monsieur Manceau, in the middle of his speech, with the town council around him, while in the foreground was a dense crowd. As they looked up at the balcony they all had their backs to the camera, all, that is, except one. He was a little boy of between six and eight, whom a woman in black was holding by the hand. The photographer's activities must have interested him for he had turned to watch and his face stood out clearly in the crowd.

'The little boy in the garden!' Marion cried.

'And the woman is probably Madame Bollaert,' Fernand added.

'Very probably,' Monsieur Théo replied. 'All the prisoner could deduce from it was that his son was out and about in Louvigny. He sent the paper back to Rat and asked him to make some delicate inquiries. Rat took me into his confidence right away and from then on we began our investigations. It was a ticklish business. For one thing we hadn't got to let the couple who had adopted the boy know what was going on, and then we couldn't ask openly at the Town Hall in case they started to get suspicious. I know Inspector Sinet, I've often gone to him about my villains, and I gave him the gist of the story. Only the gist, mind you, you've got to watch that chap. With a copy of the photo, he discreetly inquired of the officials at the Town Hall and of several private people who do social work in the town, but he never succeeded in tracing the child. All he could tell us was that the verdict of the court had been confirmed and that an adoption order is never reversed. That was all, and it wasn't encouraging. Meanwhile there was this accident which cost our friend his sight. There was nothing about it in the papers, but then things like that never leak through the prison walls.'

'Where did it happen?' Fernand asked.

'In the machine shop. About twenty prisoners were working when a cylinder of liquid oxygen exploded, killing three and injuring all the others in one way or another. It was a terrible retribution. You see the ogre had pretended to be a blind man to put the police off the scent, and now the disguise had become all too real. It's a sad story! We heard about it two months later when Rat had a letter from his old cell-mate. In view of what had happened to him, the Parole Board decided to remit the rest of his sentence, and to free him. They set, as well, the guilt of his child-stealing against the upheaval the loss of his own son caused him. He was a fine present! The poor devil arrived out of the blue and I had to put him up with the others. The thought that his boy was somewhere in the district made him quite desperate and it was all his idea to go to these lengths to find him again. He had to attract the child's attention without frightening him, and to get in touch with him behind the adoptive parents' backs. How was he to make himself known? It wasn't exactly easy. The last time he saw his son, the little boy had been about six and at that age you've a short memory. The blind man had changed a lot physically: prison had aged him, his accident had disfigured him, and the dark glasses supplied the final touch which made him unrecognizable. It was then that he had the idea of letting the little boy know who he was by using things that would have stuck in his memory. He bored us for hours with his descriptions of his black dog, Toby, his little boy's favourite pet. And then he went back to his accordion and remembered an old tune his son had loved and which he had played often in happier days – *Pour deux sous d'amour.*'

'You don't turn into a street musician overnight,' Marion observed.

'No, you certainly don't,' said Monsieur Théo. 'And that's just where Fate caught up with him. He had taken great pains over his one and only crime, and the disguise enabled him to keep watch without drawing unwelcome attention to himself. Nobody would suspect a blind man, playing his accordion at the street corner, of planning a terrible crime. Then bang! The accident in prison, the early release and he found himself forced to wear this sinister disguise for good and all. We started by getting hold of your Nanar. He filled Toby's description well enough as to size and general appearance, and a good dip in a dye-bath did the trick. Then we worked out this plan of exploration to cover the whole town, not leaving out the smallest block of houses. Relying on our one clue, the photograph, there was a fair chance that the little boy did live in Louvigny with a fairly well-to-do family. We took the chance, but it never entered our heads that someone else would recognize the blind man.'

'The Pierce brothers?' said Marion.

Monsieur Théo smiled.

'However complicated a problem may seem to be,' he said, 'it is only soluble if you tackle it from certain angles. The simplest approach often gives the quickest solution, rather than make up a mystery where one doesn't exist. If we had had the sense to read the newspaper reports of the case we should have thought of Monsieur Bollaert by deduction and that would have saved us a deal of time and trouble. Can't you guess?'

The two children shook their heads.

'Two truck drivers who cornered the ogre somewhere between Angoulême and La Rochefoucauld in the Charente – were the Pierce brothers! Motorists throughout France had been warned a week before to look out for the pretended blind man. He had left the kidnapped child in a church porch, since it hindered his escape, but he had been foolish enough to keep his dog, just as compromising a companion. It was hardly safe to be seen out with a black dog at the time. As the Pierce brothers were passing a small car driven by a man with a two-day growth of beard they noticed Toby lying on the back seat. There was a ten-million-franc reward going so it was worth taking more than a glance at any suspicious characters. The Pierce brothers managed to force the car in to the side of the road and that was that. He tried to put up a fight but a couple of toughs like them were too much for him. Later on they had to give evidence at the ogre's trial and their boss came with them to watch. Now Monsieur Bollaert is a very decent person. He took a deep interest in what in the end would happen to the little boy, whose mother had just died, now that his father might well spend years in prison. He and Madame Bollaert had no children of their own, and so they adopted him, settling in Louvigny and doing their best not to draw attention to their child or to his father's shameful past. There was no guarantee that the kidnapper had not got friends and, despite his heavy sentence, a man with so black a past was a real fear for the future. You can imagine how terrified they must have been when the Pierce brothers told them the blind man was actually in Louvigny. Monsieur Bollaert could take no legal action against him without upsetting the boy's future and his own peace of mind. That explains their panic and their moonlight flit to what they thought was a secure hiding-place in that forgotten street.'

Monsieur Théo stopped speaking for a moment. Dusk was drawing in over the town. The flowers in his garden were in bloom and they gave off a wonderful countryside scent. People laughed as they passed down the Rue des Estaffiers. Monsieur Théo's four thieves were home from work and were deep in an uproarious game of dice on the paved courtyard. The faithful Sacco sat in a corner under the mournful gaze of Nanar, peeling a bucketful of potatoes. Suddenly, from the depths of the barn, came the muted strains of the accordion. Marion looked round.

'That shows he's getting over it,' Monsieur Théo said in relief. 'At first he wouldn't face up to things, but now he has come to grips with the harsh facts of his position.'

'What are you going to do?' Fernand asked him.

'I'll see Monsieur Bollaert and do my best to set his mind at rest. He's quite within his rights to refuse to allow the man anywhere near his adopted son, but I may be able to persuade him to let the blind man meet the boy for a minute or two. That's all he needs to regain his confidence and his will to live.'

Marion smiled sadly.

'You must never give up hope in human kindness,' she said, looking at Monsieur Théo.

He walked over to the gate with the children.

'Be careful what you say,' he advised them. 'Make up some story for your friends. Not that I don't trust them, but there are nasty-minded people in this town who'd like nothing better than to vent their spite on a defenceless man.'

As they turned the corner of the Impasse des Otages Marion and Fernand pulled up breathless with shocked surprise. Their eight companions were lined up against the wall at the end like so many hostages. Inspector Sinet was going from one to the other brandishing a photograph and volleying them, luckily, only with questions.

'Have you seen this boy anywhere before? Where? When? Under what circumstances?'

'Don't know him,' Juan, Tatave, Bonbon, Criquet, Berthe, and Mélie answered in succession.

Marion was impressed by the complete spirit of togetherness which pervaded the gang and enabled them to put so successful a face on the most unexpected turn of events.

There was, too, a real joke about it all. Everything was finished, explained, understood, and here was this policeman, a lover of long-drawn-out games of 'belote', still at the most elementary stage of his investigations. Fernand and Marion crept up behind the Inspector's back and were within arm's reach unobserved. They were both enjoying the scene immensely, but Zidore scared them badly. He unhurriedly stretched out his hand, took the photograph delicately between forefinger and thumb, and held it, frowning, at various distances from his pointed nose.

'I'm sorry,' he said, 'but I'm rather short-sighted.'

Zidore's puzzled expression suddenly cleared in an ecstatic grin.

'Oh, Mister Inspector, sir,' he squawked, twisting his hands. 'It's not fair to tease us so. What a pretty little boy you were when you were eight years old!'

And he cleverly dodged Sinet's swipe. The exasperated policeman now stood in front of Gaby and showed him the photograph.

'Of course I know the boy,' Gaby retorted confidently. 'We all know him. If you turn round you'll see him.'

The Inspector spun round on his heel and nearly fell over backward. There stood the expressionless Fernand in front of him. Marion herself was momentarily struck by his real resemblance to the boy in the garden. He had the same slim figure, the same blue eyes and even the same lock of fair hair tumbling down on to his forehead.

'Is it really you?' Inspector Sinet asked amazed.

Young Fernand was a sensible boy and little inclined to leg-pulling: but this was too good an opportunity to miss.

'Of course it is! That's my mother's son all right!' he answered without the flicker of a smile. 'It was taken two years ago, at the official opening of the new Town Hall.

Do you think I'd forget? Not likely, you don't get your picture in the paper every day of the week.'

'Who is the lady holding your hand?'

'The sister-in-law of my Uncle Cyprien's brother, Madame Honorine Faifeux, my aunt, of course, the one who lives in Lorraine,' Fernand answered in the same tone of voice. 'Mother Nono as we call her at home.'

In his anger Inspector Sinet hurled his hat on the ground and revealed a head prematurely thinned by the cares of unsuccessful investigations and those of his twice-daily game of cards. The Ten were relieved to see him go, but they were grateful, too, for his interference had sent their morale soaring.

Marion silenced their laughter by shaking a threatening finger at the wilder spirits.

'The case of the blind man has been solved, thanks to us,' she said gravely. 'It's over. After this evening we shan't mention it again. Monsieur Théo has asked me to thank you and to tell you if he needs us again he'll let you know. Anyone got any questions?'

They all had, plenty, but when Marion promised in that tone of voice to answer, you took good care not to ask. Little Bonbon was the only one who seemed dissatisfied with so sudden a conclusion to the case.

'I'm still a bit puzzled about one thing,' he said seriously. 'I'd like to have it out with Spare-a-copper.'

'No time like the present!' laughed Gaby, extinguishing him under the battered old hat the Inspector had forgotten.

They led him away like this to the sandpit at Villemarie and sent him tobogganing down the slope with the old hat on his head. Inspector Bonbon even kept it on when he bathed. That evening they all concentrated on enjoying themselves.

CHAPTER 15

The Fourteenth of July

CIRCUMSTANCES forced Marion to tell Gaby what had
happened. Three of them were now in the secret. Then
Gaby, whose particular friend was Zidore, whispered to
him the full details of what they were now calling 'Case
No. 2, the Blind Man'. In less than twenty-four hours, Zidore had no less confidentially told his partner-in-crime,
Juan. The ties of the Faubourg-Bacchus made the gipsy boy
pass the news on to Criquet Lariqué, and that kept him
awake three nights running. To relieve his overwrought
feelings the Negro told it all to fat Tatave, augmented with
sundry bloodthirsty details and one of the wild animal
stories of which he had an extensive collection. In the next
fifteen minutes, Tatave, under the seal of secrecy, had con-
fided to Berthe and Mélie that the blind man had once been
a big-game hunter in darkest Africa where he had had the
unpleasant habit of kidnapping pairs of piccaninnies from
the nearest village to use as live bait. At the end of the line
was the unfortunate Bonbon. He received the glad tidings
from the two girls with the benefit of all the additions made
to the original story. He could not make head or tail of it,
so matters remained much as they had been. In short, by
the week's end everybody knew what had happened, but
each pretended to the other not to know, while the blind
man dropped from their conversation as Marion had advised.

In any case the Phantom had abruptly gone out of circulation. It was not unexpected, but the Ten missed him enor-
mously after their six weeks' continuous watch over him.

Marion twice visited Number 58, Rue des Estaffiers. Monsieur Théo was pleased to see her, and his lodgers gave her a welcome. The blind man was still there, tapping his way through the chores of the reformed thieves' household. He would play his accordion all day long and occasionally come out of his customary morose silence.

Monsieur Théo had been to see Monsieur Bollaert, as he said he would, to try to make him change his mind. But the haulage contractor had been inflexible. Monsieur Théo readily admitted that the little boy in the garden stood to lose everything by learning who his real father was and that the latter would only be more deeply upset by a meeting as painful as it would be incoherent.

'How's he taking it?' Marion asked.

'Better than we expected,' was Monsieur Théo's reply. 'But he sometimes gets moods either of black depression or of unreasoned rage when he does nothing but curse and jeer at us. The other evening we were on the verge of throwing him out, dog, accordion, and all. Luckily Nanar was there. You'd think that dog understood him better than any of us. He's only to lay his head on his knee and his master calms down at once. The blind man told us that if ever he lost the dog, he'd have nothing left to live for.'

Monsieur Théo thoughtfully rubbed the back of his head.

'The devil of it is,' he added, 'that your Nanar eats like a horse. That dog's always got his jaws open.'

This amused Marion immensely.

'The blind man ought occasionally to make some effort at least to pay for his food,' she said. 'You'll have to persuade him to go out again and play on the Place du Marché, or somewhere else. Folk in Louvigny aren't that mean, you know, and if he played in the right spots, and we'd show him the best ones, he could raise a steady little income in the region of five or six hundred francs a day.'

She paused and smiled into space.

'The truth is,' she said, 'we're beginning to miss him rather.'

'I'll tell him,' Monsieur Théo promised. 'Maybe it'll help to bring him out of his shell.'

As she was leaving Marion ran into big Sacco. He was just coming out of the kitchen, saucepan in hand, with the cat at his heels. She belonged to the house and was a superb creature.

Marion was always forgiving, but the scab on her knee made her remember being shoved on to a certain deserted roadway in the Quartier-Neuf.

'Someone pinched a six-pound ham out of the big butcher's shop in the Rue Piot,' she said point-blank as she faced him.

Big Sacco blushed and stood there tongue-tied. In the background the others chuckled.

'It wasn't him,' Monsieur Théo assured Marion, 'the only thieves in the place are that fat cat and that pig Nanar. They're like brothers when it comes to breaking into my larder. Be off with you!'

Louvigny's humblest homes were beginning to discuss the seaside and holidays with or without pay. One day Tatave and Bonbon proclaimed their imminent departure for a distant holiday camp. The others were rather jealous and, as they awaited the great day, they loaded the two deserters with sarcastic and mock-horrific advice. But the Louvrier brothers never left.

'Hi, you campers!' Gaby teased them one day when they were bathing. 'Look at the embankment! You've missed your old train!'

And so it was. All day long, trains packed with holiday-makers crawled past the sandpit at Villemarie, as though to inspect the little resort with its visitors shouting and splashing in the muddy waters.

'You make me laugh with your holidays!' Zidore would bawl at the mermen of Louvigny-on-Sea. 'I'll spend mine on the pavement of the Rue du Malassis, like every summer. You're much better off at home.'

And seizing Berthe, Mélie, Criquet, or Bonbon by the scruff of the neck he would make them, then and there, drink his health in local water. Little Bonbon would not be parted from Inspector Sinet's battered hat and, proud as a peacock, he strolled the streets of the town in the shade of the headpiece which had absorbed so much of the detective's anxious sweat.

But such fun and laughter served only to bridge a gap which none of the Ten admitted, but which left them thoughtful and often bored, for they really missed the blind man. Juan and Fernand one day prowled around the Rue César-Santini. The garage was closed up. The crimson lorries, too, had gone out of circulation. Astonished, the two Holmeses furtively explored the forgotten street. There was the same silence and emptiness as well. Monsieur Bollaert had packed up and, with his wife, his adopted son, and his two partners, the Pierce brothers, had left for an unknown destination where they could at last enjoy real happiness as a family.

Then the Ten thought they had found a diversion in that annual occurrence, the Sweepstake, and it nearly looked like being Case No. 3. The ticket winning the top prize of seventy-five million francs had been sold to a single buyer[1] by the Bar-Tabac in the Grand-Rue. All the hard-ups in Louvigny-Triage and Louvigny-Cambrouse tried feverishly to discover who the lucky individual was. But the

1. In France tickets for the Sweepstake can be bought in quarter or half shares, or even in tenth shares.

latter was no fool, for he took good care not to admit his luck or to give it away by a suspicious burst of generosity.

Gaby at once had his bloodhounds out.

Broken in by their forty-five days' concentrated shadowing, the children scattered in all directions to pick up the trail of the multi-millionaire among the district's twelve thousand inhabitants, and to shout his name from the housetops. Housewives could no longer buy a joint or a fowl without being noticed by a suspicious eye and reported to the chief detective ten minutes later at his office on the Place du Marché opposite the Café Parisien.

'The miser!' said Gaby, enraged by useless information that always kept sending them off on false trails. 'He's not satisfied with seventy-five million! He must be sitting on it to see if it'll hatch out into more. What would you do, Tatave, if you found seventy-five million in the dining-room cupboard?'

'I'd be off to that holiday camp like a shot!' the would-be camper answered bitterly. He had not got over the disappointment. 'And be blowed to the rest of you!'

'What about you, Zidore?'

'Me?' said the Bulldog Drummond of the Rue du Malassis. 'Oh, I'd take seventy-five years' holiday. Too bad if I died flat broke in my nineties. The parish would have to bury me!'

'Seventy-five million!' muttered Marion, whose generous heart overflowed with schemes to help others. 'That wouldn't be nearly enough for all I'd like to do.'

But despite their constant vigilance and their boldest moves the Fourteenth of July came and still the winner of the Sweepstake kept his pile and his identity intact. Gaby gave them the day off. Berthe and Mélie stopped spying on the big butcher's shop in the Rue Piot and Zidore left his post outside Béquillard's shop in whose window gleamed a brand-new motor scooter.

The National Holiday was celebrated in different ways in Louvigny according to the importance of the streets, the whim of their inhabitants, and the generosity of the café proprietors. There was dancing on the Place du Marché and in the Rue de Paris where two local bands set people's feet tapping and blasted the peace of the surrounding streets with their noise.

On Gaby's orders, Marion had turned the gang's funds, seven hundred and seventy francs, into rockets, bangers, crackers, and other fireworks. After a successful trial, the bulk of the explosives was saved for later on.

Being slightly off the beaten track, the Rue des Petits-Pauvres only felt the backwash of the celebrations and when night fell it was as melancholy as usual. It had been a glorious day and it was still light at ten o'clock. But the Ten had to be home by midnight and so they gathered in the street without delay to celebrate, after their own fashion, the Fall of the Bastille. The first firework went off like a dream under fat Madame Babin's skirts as she sat in her doorway and instantly earned Tatave the finest pair of cuffs on the ear he had had in his life.

Marion touched off a Bengal light and it filled the street with its glorious greenish glow for some minutes, and produced admiring cries from all along the houses. Bonbon ran up and down the street like a madman setting off his bangers against the closed doors. Meanwhile Gaby, Zidore, and Fernand had been preparing a miniature display in Monsieur Douin's front garden, by kind permission of the owner. People had come up from the end of the road to watch the grand finale and they gathered on the opposite pavement, chatting languidly in the twilight. But their hearts were not in it.

At eleven o'clock, Gaby, raised to the rank of master of ceremonies, lit the first fuse in an eager silence. It all fell flat. The fireworks must have been very old stock, for the two rockets spat a few miserable sparks as they hissed over the tops of the roofs and the biggest Bengal light poured a stream of black smoke over the watchers.

'Try the candle,' Monsieur Douin called, bitterly disappointed for the children's sake.

Gaby put a match under the Roman candle. It went off with a *phutt* and did succeed in raising a laugh.

'Don't worry,' Monsieur Douin said to Gaby, 'we've still got the Catherine wheel, and that should be the best of the batch.'

The Catherine wheel took two minutes to catch light and then it blew up like a bomb, wreaking havoc among Monsieur Douin's rambler roses. The people in the street light-heartedly whistled at the firework lighter.

Gaby was on the point of cursing the Republic and its day of glory when suddenly from the corner of the Rue Cécile came the muted sounds of an accordion. The touch of music was enough to transform the children's world and in a flash the summer's evening seemed brighter.

'The blind man!' Fernand called.

But Marion was already running with the others towards the end of the street.

Sitting on his camp-stool on the edge of the pavement, the Phantom had swung into one of the Viennese waltzes in his repertoire.

'Here we are,' Marion murmured as she pulled up in front of him. 'The whole gang!'

The blind man slowly nodded his head, and for the first time since he had come to the town, he smiled.

There were no fairy-lights or Chinese lanterns in the Rue des Petits-Pauvres, but one by one the lights came on in the houses round the cross-roads, marking out a circle of gold in which the first couples were already dancing to the rhythmic beat of the accordion. Criquet Lariqué ceremoniously led Mélie Babin on to the floor, followed next by Berthe and Bonbon, and then by Fernand and the girl with the dogs, her face beaming happily. Zidore

and Tatave gave a disorderly display of rock 'n' roll.

Down to the little Bar de l'Auvergnat went one of the householders from the cross-roads. He had not won the Sweepstake, but none the less he returned with crates of beer and lemonade and set up a free bar on two tables in his front garden. There was plenty for everybody and for the street musician who tirelessly played from waltz to rhumba and back again.

The tide of happiness that swelled the town had at last flowed into the Rue des Petits-Pauvres and all could freely plunge into it. Below the dark glasses the blind man's face smiled all the time as it poured with sweat. Strangers came up to give him a friendly thump on the shoulder and to wish him well. From that night forward all was forgiven and forgotten. The worst might have happened but in spite of everything it was still possible to recover a honest livelihood. On all sides laughter mingled with the inspired strains of the accordion. One last flourish swirled madly round the man in black who had just earned the freedom of the town by making the folk of the Rue des Petits-Pauvres dance.

It was late when the children left, after saying delighted good nights to the blind man. Marion and Fernand lingered as the lights around went out and the man clumsily strapped up his old accordion.

'I wonder if you really can't see at all?' Marion suddenly said as she watched the blind man packing up.

'Some days I see better than others,' he answered with a chuckle. 'But I shall never see well enough to see your face.'

Marion could guess at the regret behind those words of resignation. She was just going when the blind man called her back.

'Here!' he said. 'I think this is yours.'

And he slipped into her hand the little gilt brooch she had

lost a fortnight before in the empty road in the Quartier-Neuf. For a moment Marion did not know what to say, but the cheap piece of jewellery became doubly dear to her.

'You'll come back?' she murmured.

'Every day,' said the blind man.

Marion had never told a big lie. She did so for the first time, but it was a noble lie.

'Monsieur Bollaert's come back,' she said abruptly. 'He and his wife and the boy are living in a place in the Quartier-Neuf. Don't go and tell Monsieur Théo I've told you this. We've worked something out between us.'

'What?' the blind man asked, rooted to the spot.

'There used to be ten of us,' Marion answered. 'From now on there'll be eleven. You can't see me and you won't see the eleventh, but you'll hear him laughing, singing, and playing around you like the rest of us. You mustn't call him by name, and you mustn't speak to him either. You'll only scare him with your stories of the old days. But he'll be there, every day, one of us.'

Fernand stood slightly to one side, not speaking and with a half-smile on his face, ready to play this new part Marion had invented.

'What more could you hope for?' she asked in the end.

'Nothing!' whispered the blind man. 'That's all I want.'

And he walked slowly towards the Place du Marché whistling the only tune he had not played that evening – *Pour deux sous d'amour.*

It was early next morning, when Bonbon went out to fetch the milk for breakfast, that he noticed his dream Cadillac parked outside the Bar-Tabac in the Grand-Rue. A splendid open blue and white car, with masses of gleaming chromium-plate, an absolute beauty.

A chauffeur in a white livery with dark-blue facings,

wearing a cap fit for an admiral, sat at the wheel. Bonbon carefully walked round and round the miracle, asking himself if he was still asleep and imagining the heavenly noise such an engine would make when it pulled away from the pavement.

'That's just the car,' he told himself, 'for the stingy multi-millionaire who's hiding in Louvigny. I'll wait!'

He did not have to stand about for long. The Bar-Tabac was crowded with jovial characters who had celebrated the Fourteenth of July too well and were now breakfasting off smoked sausage washed down with white wine. Suddenly there was a great hubbub at the door and Bonbon saw the tramp Spare-a-copper come out amid a burst of cheering, large as life, dirty, hairy, and ragged, carrying those badges of poverty, his bundle and knapsack.

The chauffeur jumped smartly out of the Cadillac, opened the rear door and cap in hand bowed low to the beggar. Bonbon rubbed his eyes hard, but the vision did not disappear. He could not be mistaken.

With immense dignity, Spare-a-copper got into the incomparable Cadillac and relaxed luxuriously upon the pearl-grey cushions, while the smart chauffeur respectfully clicked shut the door.

Bonbon came close, gaping. He still could not believe his eyes. But it really was Spare-a-copper, and the dirty old object was sprawled negligently on the spotless upholstery of the back seat. Out of a pocket he drew a cigar as long and as fat as a truncheon, lit it with greedy puffs and stared ferociously at Bonbon above the flame of his lighter. Then he snapped his fingers in a most provocative fashion under Bonbon's very nose and in a voice still husky from the previous evening's libations he brought the curtain down with his order to his chauffeur.

'The Ritz, Adolphe, and hurry!'

The Cadillac purred away, leaving the baby of the gang open-mouthed on the pavement.

'Spare-a-copper really had me,' he later admitted to his friends. 'Not half he didn't. Who'd have thought it was him who won the lottery!'

THE AUTHOR

Paul Berna was born at Hyeres in 1913. He was the youngest son of a large, noisy, and quarrelsome family where everybody had a good deal of fun. He spent the whole of his childhood in the South of France, and though circumstances have forced him to spend a lot of time elsewhere he has always been very attached to this part of the country.

He went to school in Toulon and later at Aix, where he did very well, passing his pre-university exam with credit. His great interest in books and literature of every kind went hand in hand with an enthusiasm for football and swimming. After leaving school he did a two-year apprenticeship at a Paris Bank. This was followed by a number of jobs, none of which really appealed to him. After the Second World War he was offered an administrative job in the Post Office.

In spite of his professional occupations he has always been interested in young people and their books. Indeed, all his works show that he has a remarkable insight into the mind of the modern child.

A Hundred Million Francs, *Flood Warning*, and *The Knights of King Midas* are all available in Puffins.

In 1960 he married Saint-Marcoux who is well known for her novels for older girls.

*You can read about some
other Puffin Books on the
following pages*

THE BRUMBY

Mary Elwyn Patchett

The Brumby of this story was a wild Australian stallion, born near the home of a lonely boy, and capturing his imagination with such intensity that he could think and dream of nothing but one day building up a herd of sturdy silver brumbies.

But to the Australian stockmen among whom he lived all brumbies were wild, vicious, untameable animals fit only to be hunted, and young Joey had to endure seeing his beloved foal grow up into a savage outlaw and finally a killer. Nevertheless his dream comes true, although not quite as he'd imagined it.

JENNINGS GOES TO SCHOOL

Anthony Buckeridge

'Jennings, what does a bat do in winter?'
'It – er – it splits if you don't oil it, sir.'

Even if he isn't always as attentive as his master would wish, J. T. C. Jennings is a well-meaning, cheerful and obliging boy, and it seems surprising that his arrival at Linbury Court Preparatory School should cause life there to become so hectic, hilarious, and generally unpredictable.

His intentions are always good and there is no doubt that his serious-minded friend Darbishire ought to be a soothing influence, but between them they are responsible for a number of hair-raising incidents, including the false fire alarm and the Poisonous Spider.

MAGNOLIA BUILDINGS

Elizabeth Stucley

Val 'dashed up the first flight, braced at any moment for a
kick from the shadows or one of Nap's famous springs. At
the moment he did not feel a debonair gangster any more,
but a frightened hungry boy who was up against heavy
odds'. This is part of what life is like in Magnolia Buildings
where twelve-year-old Val lives with his Mum and Dad,
two sisters, fourteen-year-old Ally, who longs for glamour,
eleven-year-old Doreen, who longs for a scholarship, and his
brother Len, who longs for a pet. All the Berners live life to
the hilt in their own way, but they haven't much money to
do it on, and sometimes the shortage leads them into trouble
and temptation.

THE TWENTY-TWO LETTERS

Clive King

Long ago, 1500 years before Christ was born, when King
Minos of Crete still worshipped the bull, when the Eastern
Mediterranean was divided into many unstable little states,
and Egyptian writing was a sacred and secret cult, Resh the
master builder lived in the city of Byblos with his three sons
and his daughter.

Resh was very busy building a new palace for the King,
but his three sons went off in different directions. All the time
they were away their father and sister Beth were waiting
anxiously for their safe return with the presents they should
give the King on his Day of Offering. But despite the un-
heard-of way Aleph sent a message warning the King of his
enemies' approach, nothing could prevent the disaster which
the strange man from the eastern land of Chaldea had fore-
told.

A PUFFIN ORIGINAL

MASTER OF MORGANA
Allan Campbell McLean

A story set in the Isle of Skye. Niall, the sixteen-year-old hero, attempts to discover the reason for his brother's nearly fatal accident at the salmon fisheries, and finds himself caught up in ghost hunting, treasure hunting, smuggling and attempted murder.

STARMAN JONES
Robert A. Heinlein

This is a story of the world in 200 years' time, when rockets to the moon are as commonplace as trains to Ealing, and weekly space ships loaded with supplies and settlers leave for the planets as regularly as our ships now sail to Europe.

Max Jones is an orphan who dreams of being an astrogator. He insinuates himself aboard the 'Asgard', but there is a mistake in calculation and instead of making the planned leap of ninety-seven light years, they enter another galaxy and are obliged to land on an unknown star. This turns out to be inhabited by flying jellyfish and a strange kind of centaur who use men as beasts of burden. Max and Ellie, the girl he wants to marry, are captured and there are some hair-raising adventures and dramatic decisions to be made before Max is able to make the calculations which will take them back through the 'Hole' to their known planet.

For readers of eleven upwards who are interested in the world of the future.